TREASURY of
Christmas Stories

TREASURY of
Christmas Stories

Edited by ANN McGOVERN

Illustrated by David Lockhart

FOUR WINDS PRESS • NEW YORK

Published by Four Winds Press
A Division of Scholastic Magazines, Inc., New York, N.Y.
Copyright © 1960 by Scholastic Magazines, Inc.
Printed in the United States of America.

ACKNOWLEDGMENTS

Ashes of the Christmas Tree by Yetza Gillespie from *Good Housekeeping*. Copyright 1946 by the Hearst Corporation. Reprinted by permission of Mrs. Ramona Cramer.

Christmas from the book AROUND AND ABOUT by Marchette Chute. Copyright 1946 by Marchette Chute. Published 1957 by E. P. Dutton & Co., Inc. and reprinted with their permission.

Christmas Every Day by William Dean Howells. Reprinted from *St. Nicholas Magazine*. Courtesy of Appleton-Century-Crofts.

A Christmas Gift for the General by Jeanette Nolan from *Child Life Magazine*. Copyright 1937, 1965 by Rand McNally & Company.

Christmas Tree by Aileen Fisher. Copyright 1946 by Aileen Fisher. Reprinted from CHRISTMAS PLAYS AND PROGRAMS by permission of Plays, Inc., Publishers.

Day Before Christmas from the book RHYMES ABOUT THE COUNTRY by Marchette Chute. Copyright 1941 by Marchette Chute. Reprinted by permission of the author.

The Gift of St. Nicholas from AMERICAN MYTHS AND LEGENDS by Charles M. Skinner, published by J. B. Lippincott Co. The version used here is reprinted from Anne Malcolmson's YANKEE DOODLE'S COUSINS, copyright 1941 by Anne B. Malcolmson. This selection reprinted by permission of Houghton Mifflin Company.

Golden Cobwebs from STORY TELLER POEMS by Rowena Bennett. Copyright 1948 by Holt, Rinehart and Winston, Inc. Reprinted by permission of the author.

How Santa Claus Found the Poorhouse by Sophie Swett from HAPPY CHRISTMAS, edited by Claire H. Bishop, published by Stephen Daye Press. Copyright 1956 by Stephen Daye Press.

The Jar of Rosemary by Maud Lindsay from THE STORY TELLER by Maud Lindsay. Reprinted by permission of Lothrop, Lee & Shepard Co., Inc.

CONTENTS

TREASURY of
Christmas Stories

Secret In The Barn

By Anne Wood

It's nearly Christmas — it's Christmas Eve!
And it's snowing all over the place,
The roof of the barn is sugary white —
Its eaves are lined with lace.
Our cornfield looks like a polar bear rug —
The silos wear marshmallow hats,
The kittens are into snow to their chins
And the cows all sport white spats.

Dad cut a pine —
From our own backwoods —
Where it stood all heavy with snow,

And we've decked it with lights
And tinsel trim
Till you can't see the tree for the glow!

My mom's in the kitchen,
She's baking mince pies
And gingerbread boys
With raisins for eyes.

And Grandma's in charge
Of other
Things
Like hanging the stockings, and
Mending mittens, and
Scolding my brothers for
Stealing raisins, and
Feeding the kitten, and
Pouring tea
When the
Kettle
Sings . . .

Snowflake white,
snowflake bright —
Who'll grant us
the wishes
we wish
tonight?

1

My brother Ben wants a collie pup;
Bill hopes for a three-geared bike —
Jim dreams of a lo-ong electric train
with —

double switches,
and tunnels and bridges
for hills and ditches —
A train that'll run
without any hitches
at any speed you like.

I'm twelve.
I'm Louise —
And a girl, of course.
I'm hardest to please
'Cause I've begged
On my *knees*
All
Year
— for a horse . . . .

Snowflake bright, snowflake white —
First snowflake I ask tonight —
I beg with all my main and might —
Give me the wish I wish tonight!

Last night I was thinking of . . . well . . . of *horses*
And, oh, it was hard to sleep!
"Louise, my child," said Grandma at last,
"Have you tried counting sheep?"

So — I tried and *tried* to imagine sheep
But what did I see instead?
Horses!! — Black, brown, chestnut, bay,
          Palomino, pinto, roan and gray,
          Strawberry sorrels with manes of red,
          Galloping, galloping past my bed!

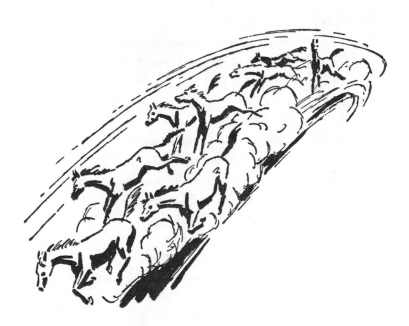

"Still no luck?" said Mom.
"Then I'll teach you a game.
You know, everyone's Christmas
Isn't the same.

3

If we think of people whose Christmas must be
Different from Christmas in our family —
And *you* think of a few

    and *I* think of a few
        you'll feel pretty sleepy
           before we are through!"

    "My turn?" I asked. "Well, the boys and I
    Spend every Christmas here,
    But an Army Captain's children
    Have to move most every year.
They've Christmas first in Oregon —
And next in North Dakota,
Or Iowa or Idaho,
Or Maine or Minnesota . . . .
And Mom, think of the astronauts
Whose children know that soon
Their fathers may be celebrating
Christmas on the moon!"

Said Mom, "When the Cannonball Special goes by
To the city and back again,
I like to think of the engineer
At the throttle of that train.

Does a sprig of mistletoe hang in his cab
As he roars down the rails like a rocket?
Is a note saying 'Wish you were with us, Dad!'
Tucked in his work-shirt pocket?

"And think, Louise, of your Uncle," she mused,
"Who works on the telephone truck!
Why, every blessed Christmas day
It seems to be his luck
To be perched like a jay on a telephone pole
Making a line repair,
So folks can phone to faraway friends
And say, 'How's your Christmas there?' "

... I was getting pretty sleepy now,
But I tried to keep on with the game ....
"It's Christmas at all the hospitals,
But the nurses work, just the same ....
They put holly bouquets
on the dinner trays,
and there's
turkey to eat,
of course,
and ...
Mother ... will I
won't I ...
will I ...
won't I ...
get my ...
horse ....?"

Snowflake, snowflake, snowflake white —
Making magic in the night —
I hope it's so — I hope I'm right —
I hope my wish comes true tonight!

6

All day I've been told "You're imagining things!
Calm down! It's not what it seems!"
But I can't help believing, from clues all around,
That the barn hides the steed of my dreams!
I am certain, for instance, a horse passed our yard
In the darkness a few nights ago.
Who'd ever mistake the thumpety thump
Of the hoofs of a horse in the snow?

When I heard it, I ran like a deer to the door —
But Mom suddenly started to scold me!
"Shut the door, silly girl!" (That's not like her at *all*!)
And the very next morning Dad told me:
"The barn has been made out of bounds now, Louise,
For you and the boys — and I *mean* it."
*Since then we can hear there is something alive
In the barn — though no one has seen it.*

Of course, Ben believes it's a dog, and it's true
Dad said he could have one some day.

7

But let me ask this: Would a collie munch oats?
Would he whinny? Or stamp? Or need hay?
Bill thinks they are putting together his bike
With its gears and its searchlight and bell.
(Hush! Did you hear it? I did! A horse sneezed.
Well it did — I can certainly tell!)

> Funny Grandma
> Declares:
> "Goodness gracious! What airs!
> Buy a *horse*? I must say — we are *not*
>   millionaires!"
> (But she *knows* — I can tell by the smile that
>   she wears.)

And why do my brothers all grin when I peek
At the package that's under the tree?
It's a package that's HUGE and lumpy and odd
And it seems to be marked for me.
(Jim says it isn't — he says it's the box,
From the model-train company,
                    just *crammed* with —
                            miles of tracks
                            and a modern station,

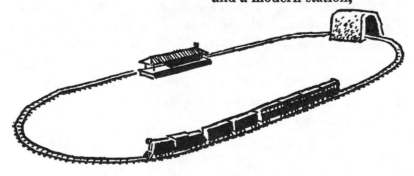

glass-domed chair-cars
for observation,
tank cars, gondolas
freighters
for mail,
sleepers, cabooses,
in perfect detail,
twin signal towers
with remote-control powers
and a thing that blows back
real smoke from the stack....)

Well, I really don't care to argue, but as sure as you
were born
The bump on the package is just the shape of a
Western saddle horn.

Snowflake,
Snowflake,
The night has descended

On all of our world
Of white.
The time
Of waiting
Will soon be ended ....
— *I'm shutting my eyes up tight!*
And I'm wishing with all my might!

Let Bill have his bicycle
Ben have his collie,

9

And astronauts find
Their moon decked in holly —
Let the engineer's Christmas
Be jolly as Jim's —
As he roars down the track
May he hum Christmas hymns!
Let my Grandma feel *young*
And let nobody dare
Ask my Uncle tomorrow
To make a repair.
To the nurses, I hope
Many patients will say,
"I am feeling so well —
Let me help *you* today!"
May the Army Post children
Rejoice in each home,
And their Christmas be merry
Wherever they roam.

A big hug-and-squeeze
I would give Mom and Dad
To remind them I'm theirs
And to show that I'm glad.

And last but not least,
If a wish works at all —
O beautiful snowflake
As softly you fall —
Keep my horse warm and safe for me
Out in his stall.

A Christmas Gift for the General

A Story of the Revolution

By Jeannette Covert Nolan

Kennet, at the window, thought that the day was not at all like Christmas. The street he looked into was silent, almost desolate; the few people passing walked quickly with bent heads, as if they were cold, or sad—

11

or both. Their feet left moist black imprints in the banked snow.

Christmas? Kennet sighed, yearning in his heart for other, better years, when peace was abroad in the land and a holiday could be celebrated in proper fashion; when Hessian troops remained across the ocean where they belonged; when the little town of Trenton was not hushed, terrified, but a pleasant place in which to live, to make merry with friends and to share presents and gay greetings. Today Kennet hadn't offered or received a single Christmas present—not one! and this, to him, seemed tragedy indeed.

He sighed, and Grandfather, hearing the mournful sound, rose from his fireside chair and hobbled over to lay a comforting hand on his shoulder.

"What ails you, lad?"

Ah, but Grandfather knew. Grandfather might be old and so crippled now by rheumatism that he must stay always indoors, crouching over the logs to warm his ancient, aching joints; yet his spirit was youthful, strong. In Grandfather's breast burned the pure flame of patriotism. He gripped Kennet's arm and sighed, too.

"Is it true," Kennet asked, turning, "as they are saying: that General Washington must lose the war?"

The old man pursed withered lips. "Lately all reports have been discouraging. The soldiers suffer from dreadful cold, from lack of food and supplies. A dark hour for our country, very dark. But," Grandfather ended

12

bravely, "there's still hope. Maybe in the spring our luck will change."

"You don't mean the Hessians will be quartered here until spring!" Kennet wailed. "Oh, but we couldn't bear it. Those harsh, impudent—"

Grandfather lifted a warning finger. Kennet must not denounce the Hessians, he said. No, they were here, occupying Trenton, taking the best of everything and living handsomely, while townsfolk skimped, pinched and went hungry. They couldn't be ousted; therefore they must be tolerated—the Hessians, King George's hireling troops.

"Don't grumble," Grandfather advised.

But as he hobbled painfully back to his chair, he muttered under his breath that he would give his own life gladly, poor old thing that it was, if only with it he might aid the cause of freedom.

Presently Kennet put on his cap and leather jacket. Carefully, so that Grandfather would not notice, he got a loaf of bread from the cupboard box, a scrap of dried meat from the shelf. He opened the door then and slipped out.

On the porch's narrow step was Toby, the black hound. At sight of his master, the big fellow reared up on hind legs, barked joyously and began the comical dance which Kennet had taught him.

"No, Toby," Kennet said gravely. "This isn't the time for tricks."

Toby had the most beautiful eyes in the world and a

13

wide mouth stretched in an incessant, amiable grin. He had intelligence, too, beneath that satiny black skull of his. At the boy's command he dropped down obediently on four feet again, wagging his tail.

The dog beside him, Kennet walked to the river and stood for a moment staring out over the ice-choked water. On the far shore, dim behind curtains of falling snow, were the rolling Pennsylvania hills. Nearer, on the Jersey side, were the piers and docks, deserted and idle.

Kennet turned his back on the town. He sought a path at the water's edge. For almost a mile he trudged, winding with the river through thickets of rustling, bare-branched trees and snow-shrouded bushes, reaching at last a clearing where nestled a sturdy wooden shed with peaked roof and little windows.

Over the door was a sign. Kennet read it sorrowfully: K. Strawn & Son, Carpenters. K. Strawn?—that was Grandfather, so ill and feeble. Son—that was Father, dear Father, far from home now, serving in the Continental Army. And there was no carpentry work done here these days.

Yet the shed did hold treasure even now, and Kennet must come occasionally like this to visit it. The shed housed his boat, the roomy, iron-keeled craft which Grandfather and Father had built for him two years ago. The Madcap—that was her splendid name, lettered on her stern with yellow paint; and many a fine trip up and down the Delaware had Kennet taken in her. But that, of course, was before the war. Now The Madcap

14

was propped, high and dry, on blocks within the shed walls. He didn't know when she would be sailed again.

He unlocked the door and swung it on its rusty hinges. The interior of the shed was gloomy with shadows, chill and bleak. He lighted a candle; his breath formed a little steamy cloud above the orange flame. He set the candle on a chest and bent over his boat. With a cloth he brushed dust from the seats and polished the metal strips on the rudder. But all this he did absently. Really, he was listening, waiting; and soon he heard what he listened for—a faint yet distinct scratching on the windowpane.

A signal.

Kennet strode to the door, pushed it cautiously ajar. A man entered. It was he, the ragged stranger, the wanderer Kennet had met yesterday in the woods, who was so hollow-eyed, starved and mysterious. In the circle of candlelight, the man and the boy faced each other. The man was first to speak.

"So, you came!" His voice was deep and musical. "I was afraid you'd forget."

"No, I couldn't forget my solemn promise."

"And did you bring me food?"

"A snack." Kennet drew the bread and meat from his pocket. "We had nothing else."

"Excellent, my boy!" The man's eyes gleamed. "A feast!" Throwing himself on a bench, he ate ravenously.

Watching, Kennet realized how hungry this stranger must be, and wondered how many hours had passed since his last meal. A great many, probably. The man glanced up and encountered the boy's steady, sober gaze. He smiled and wiped his mouth on the back of one red, frostbitten hand.

"As delicious a dinner as I ever had," he said, stooping to caress Toby, to stroke the long velvety ears. "I thank you for your kindness."

Kennet nodded courteously. "You are welcome."

"Sit down." As the boy took a place on the bench, the man said, "Why have you befriended me? You don't know me, never laid eyes on me until twenty-four hours ago."

"It's Christmas," Kennet answered simply.

"And you observe the day with charity?"

"Yes. I know you are deserving. You are not a tramp—even though your clothes are so torn and dirty."

"My clothes are shabby, aren't they?" He flipped the sleeve of his threadbare coat. "But they'll do. I don't go about much in society. You didn't mention to anyone that you saw me?" He paused anxiously.

"Not even to my grandfather."

"Good! It's absolutely necessary that I keep under cover. Much depends on it. You'd never have seen me yesterday, if I hadn't been near perishing for food. But there you were, on the river path—and there was I, peeping out. Remember? And in a moment we had spoken, were talking like comrades, well-met! And you were promising to feed me."

16

Kennet leaned forward. "I think," he said, "you are a soldier."

"A soldier?" The man flushed. "Now why should you think—"

"My father is a soldier, and if he is hungry today, I should like to believe that someone, somewhere, is feeding—"

But here Kennet paused, for the man was frowning, putting an admonishing finger to his lips. What was that noise at the door? Why did Toby bristle and growl?

The noise again. A stamping of feet, an angry shouting. "Open! Open, in the King's name!"

The King's name? An enemy, then? A Hessian? Kennet tiptoed to the window. Yes, outside in the snow bulked a stalwart figure, a Hessian, uniformed and armed.

"Open!" With his sword, the Hessian pounded the shed door.

Kennet's breath fluttered in his throat. "What shall we do?" he whispered.

"Open, and say you are alone." Swift as lightning, the ragged stranger leaped into The Madcap, flung himself down and crawled under a strip of canvas. He was hidden; he would not be seen.

Slowly Kennet went to the door, unlocked it; he was almost thrown over backward by the violence of the Hessian's rushing entrance. He braced himself before the rude intruder; he waited.

"What are you doing here? Who are you?"

17

"Kennet Strawn. I live in Trenton with my grandfather. This is his shop."

"Who is with you?" The words were curt, accusing.

"I am alone."

"Nonsense! The door was bolted. You were speaking to someone. You came here to meet someone. Where is he?"

"No, no—"

The Hessian grimaced. Scornfully, with the toe of his shiny boot, he indicated crumbs which had fallen to the floor. "Someone has dined here."

"I carried a bit of lunch in my pocket."

The Hessian lunged and grasped the boy by the shoulder, shook him fiercely. "You lie! You're sheltering a spy. You'll pay dear for this!"

At that very instant, Toby decided to have a part in the scene. Toby had been snarling, barking. Now, jaws wide, he dashed at the ruffian who threatened his beloved master. The dog's sharp teeth caught the man's leg above the heavy boot, sank in through cloth, found the flesh. With oaths and a howl of rage and pain, the Hessian released Kennet.

"You beast!" He kicked. He struck out with his fist. He whipped the sword from his belt. The terrible, glistening blade swept upward—

"Oh, please!" Kennet moaned. "Please don't kill Toby!"

The blade poised, descended in an arc—an arc that was abruptly halted. The sword was thrust aside, clattered to the floor, as the Hessian swayed and struggled in a pair of steel-like arms.

It happened so quickly, the agile leap of the ragged stranger from his canvas cover, the Hessian's astonished outcry. And then they were lurching, tumbling, all over the room, in and out of shadow, the two big men, while Kennet gasped and Toby barked wildly.

The Hessian, after his first surprise, fought like a tiger. At last, he was subdued, he yielded.

"Quick!" the stranger muttered. "A rope. A rope."

Kennet fumbled in a chest, dragged forth a length of stout rope. They bound the Hessian with it; they rolled him into a corner.

"Now I must be off!" The stranger was mopping at

19

his forehead, which was grimy and streaked with blood. "Not a minute to lose now!"

Kennet stepped back to view the limp figure of the enemy. "He isn't dead, is he?"

"No. He's not badly hurt. But he'll be quiet for a few hours. Then he'll rouse and spread the alarm. You must go home to your grandfather—and I must get away."

"Why did you jump up? He'd never have noticed you."

"Lie there like a stick of wood and let him mistreat you and kill your dog? Oh, no! No, my friend." He patted Toby's sleek head. "I must get away," he repeated and, his frown deepening, he pointed to The Madcap. "Whose boat is this?"

"Boat?" Kennet was startled at the change of subject. "Why—why, she's mine."

"Yours, eh? Want to sell her?" He laughed on a queer note. "I've got to have this boat. I can't explain, but—well, if you won't sell her, I'll steal her."

"Steal?" Kennet echoed, dismayed. "You'd steal my boat?"

"Yes. Oh, I'm an odd fellow, no doubt of it. Here!" He dug into his pocket, extracted a handful of coins. "Money."

Kennet's brain was reeling. The events of the past hour had marched so rapidly—and certainly there was no understanding them! He felt as if he were in the midst of a crazy sort of dream where nobody behaved naturally. But he was sure of one thing: he couldn't take

money from this gallant, tattered wanderer who had risked detection, perhaps his life, for him and for Toby. The Madcap—he loved her; he couldn't sell her. He thought very hard and arrived at a decision.

"Well?" The man was jangling the coins. "Well? Am I to be a purchaser or a thief?"

Kennet swallowed a huge lump in his throat. "Take the boat. I'll give her to you—for Christmas." Hadn't he been wishing all day for the opportunity to give a Christmas present?

The man bowed. "You'll never regret your generosity. You'll help me move her?"

They worked then like beavers, knocking the blocks from under The Madcap, straining every muscle to get her out of the shed, down the slope to the river. The snow aided them; though it made their footing insecure, it formed a smooth surface on which the iron keel glided like a sled on runners. Once Kennet, pausing, remarked breathily that the river was full of floating ice, it was scarcely navigable, escape would be easier by way of the woods. But the stranger only laughed; he said he needed a boat, this boat—and he didn't mind ice.

Dusk, finally, and The Madcap launched, and her new owner bidding farewell to the old!

"Good-by, my lad. God bless you."

"Good-by." Kennet quavered. He was tired, bewildered, the afternoon had been so crowded with excitement—and perhaps he hadn't acted wisely. "Can't—can't you tell me anything about yourself?"

The stranger was standing in the boat; he looked erect, soldierly. "I'll tell you this: you think you've given me a Christmas token—really, it's for someone else. For a great man, the greatest in the world today, a man who guides your fate, and mine, and all America's. This Christmas present will be delivered to him!" He smiled into the boy's puzzled face. "Hurry home. Be silent about our adventure—and don't be amazed at anything you hear!"

Early on the morning of December twenty-sixth, 1776, while the Hessian troops in Trenton dozed after their drinking and hilarious celebration of the night before, General George Washington and his men advanced upon the town. They entered by two roads, overwhelming and seizing the garrison. For hours the streets echoed with the roar of musket and cannon—and then the Hessians surrendered.

Grandfather, huddled close to the fire, was trying to piece together shreds of rumor and gossip into a logical story.

"They say he came across the Delaware, a few boats pushing through the ice. They say a spy has been here in the neighborhood for several days, obtaining boats by one means or another; and some of 'em splintered and crashed in midstream—and some crossed in safety."

Kennet was kneeling to mend the logs, shielding his face with his palm. The Madcap, had she made the crossing safely? Oh, he hoped so! And what if General Washington had been The Madcap's passenger—that great

23

man, the greatest in the world, riding to victory in Kennet Strawn's bonny boat!

"The spy, Grandfather, was he—taken?"

"They say not. They say he's one of the General's trusted officers. A gentleman. A hero." Grandfather fondled Toby's velvet ears. "Now the tide has turned. God is with us and we will win. I may not last to see the end, myself, for I am so old. But freedom will come; it's on the way, in the air." He smiled happily. "Now I am content to die.

But Kennet did not want to die. No, no! This morning, as never before, he wanted to live—for his country.

CHRISTMAS

By Marchette Chute

My goodness, my goodness,
It's Christmas again.
The bells are all ringing.
I do not know when
I've been so excited.
The tree is all fixed,
The candles are lighted,
The pudding is mixed.

The wreath's on the door
And the carols are sung,
The presents are wrapped
And the holly is hung.
The turkey is sitting
All safe in its pan,
And I am behaving
As calm as I can.

Christmas Every Day

By W. D. Howells

The little girl came into her papa's study, as she always did Saturday morning before breakfast, and asked for a story. He tried to beg off that morning, for he was very busy, but she would not let him. So he began:

"Well, once there was a little pig—"

She put her hand over his mouth and stopped him at the word. She said she had heard little pig stories till she was perfectly sick of them.

"Well, what kind of story *shall* I tell, then?"

"About Christmas. It's getting to be the season. It's past Thanksgiving already."

"It seems to me," argued her papa, "that I've told as often about Christmas as I have about little pigs."

"No difference! Christmas is more interesting."

"Well!" Her papa roused himself from his writing by a great effort. "Well, then, I'll tell you about the little girl that wanted it Christmas every day in the year. How would you like that?"

"First-rate!" said the little girl; and she nestled into a comfortable shape in his lap, ready for listening.

"Very well, then, this little pig— Oh, what are you pounding me for?"

"Because you said little pig instead of little girl."

"I should like to know what's the difference between a little pig and a little girl that wanted it Christmas every day!"

"Papa," said the little girl, warningly, "if you don't go on, I'll *give* it to you!" And at this her papa darted off like lightning, and began to tell the story as fast as he could.

Well, once there was a little girl who liked Christmas so much that she wanted it to be Christmas every day in the year; and as soon as Thanksgiving was over she began to send postal cards to the old Christmas Fairy to ask if she mightn't have it. But the old Fairy never answered any of the postals; and, after a while, the little girl found out that the Fairy was pretty particular, and wouldn't notice anything but letters, not even correspondence cards in envelopes; but real letters on sheets of paper, and sealed outside with a monogram—or your initial, anyway. So, then, she began to send her letters; and in about three weeks—or just the day before Christmas, it was—she got a letter from the Fairy, saying she might have it Christmas every day for a year, and then they would see about having it longer.

The little girl was a good deal excited already, preparing for the old-fashioned, once-a-year Christmas that was coming the next day, and perhaps the Fairy's promise didn't make such an impression on her as it would have made at some other time. She just resolved to keep it to herself, and surprise everybody with it as it kept coming true; and then it slipped out of her mind altogether.

She had a splendid Christmas. She went to bed early, so as to let Santa Claus have a chance at the stockings, and in the morning she was up before anybody and went and felt them, and found hers all lumpy with packages of candy, and oranges and grapes, and pocketbooks and rubber balls and all kinds of small presents; and her big brother's with nothing but the tongs in them; and her young lady sister's with a new silk umbrella; and her papa's and mamma's with potatoes and pieces of coal wrapped up in tissue paper, just as they always had every Christmas. Then she waited around till the rest of the family were up, and she was the first to burst into the library, when the doors were opened, and look at the large presents laid out on the library table—books, and portfolios, and boxes of stationery, and breast-pins, and dolls, and little stoves, and dozens of handker-chiefs, and ink-stands, and skates, and snow shovels, and photograph frames, and little easels, and boxes of water-colors, and Turkish paste, and nougat, and candied cher-ries, and dolls' houses, and waterproofs—and the big Christmas tree, lighted and standing in a wastebasket in the middle.

She had a splendid Christmas all day. She ate so much candy that she did not want any breakfast; and the whole forenoon the presents kept pouring in that the express-man had not had time to deliver the night before; and she went 'round giving the presents she had got for other people, and came home and ate turkey and cranberries for dinner, and plum pudding and nuts and raisins and oranges and more candy, and then went out and coasted and came in with a stomachache, crying; and her papa said he would see if his house was turned into that sort of fool's paradise another year; and they had a light sup-per, and pretty early everybody went to bed cross.

Here the little girl pounded her papa in the back, again.

"Well, what now? Did I say pigs?"

"You made them *act* like pigs."

"Well, didn't they?"

"No matter; you oughtn't to put it into a story."

29

"Very well, then, I'll take it all out."

Her father went on:

The little girl slept very heavily, and she slept very late, but she was wakened at last by the other children dancing 'round her bed with their stockings full of presents in their hands.

"What is it?" said the little girl, and she rubbed her eyes and tried to rise up in bed.

"Christmas! Christmas! Christmas!" they all shouted, and waved their stockings.

"Nonsense! It was Christmas yesterday."

Her brothers and sisters just laughed. "We don't know about that. It's Christmas today, anyway. You come into the library and see."

Then all at once it flashed on the little girl that the Fairy was keeping her promise, and her year of Christmases was beginning. She was dreadfully sleepy, but she sprang up like a lark—a lark that had overeaten itself and gone to bed cross—and darted into the library. There it was again! Books, and portfolios, and boxes of stationery, and breast-pins—

"You needn't go over it all, Papa; I guess I can remember just what was there," said the little girl.

Well, and there was the Christmas tree blazing away, and the family picking out their presents, but looking pretty sleepy, and her father perfectly puzzled, and her

mother ready to cry. "I'm sure I don't see how I'm to dispose of all these things," said her mother, and her father said it seemed to him they had had something just like it the day before, but he supposed he must have dreamed it. This struck the little girl as the best kind of a joke; and so she ate so much candy she didn't want any breakfast, and went 'round carrying presents, and had turkey and cranberries for dinner, and then went out and coasted, and came in with a—

"Papa!"
"Well, what now?"
"What did you promise, you forgetful thing?"
"Oh! oh, yes!"

Well, the next day, it was just the same thing over again, but everybody getting crosser; and at the end of a week's time so many people had lost their tempers that you could pick up lost tempers anywhere; they perfectly strewed the ground. Even when people tried to recover their tempers they usually got somebody else's, and it made the most dreadful mix.

The little girl began to get frightened, keeping the secret all to herself; she wanted to tell her mother, but she didn't dare to; and she was ashamed to ask the Fairy to take back her gift, it seemed ungrateful and ill-bred, and she thought she would try to stand it, but she hardly knew how she could, for a whole year. So it went on and on, and it was Christmas on St. Valentine's Day, and Washington's Birthday, just the same as any day, and it didn't skip even the First of April, though everything was counterfeit that day, and that was some *little* relief.

After a while, coal and potatoes began to be awfully scarce, so many had been wrapped up in tissue paper to fool Papas and Mammas with. Turkeys got to be about a thousand dollars apiece—

"Papa!"
"Well, what?"
"You're beginning to fib."
"Well, *two* thousand, then."

And they got to passing off almost anything for tur-

keys—half-grown hummingbirds, and even rocs out of
the "Arabian Nights"—the real turkeys were so scarce.
And cranberries—well, they asked a diamond apiece for
cranberries. All the woods and orchards were cut down
for Christmas trees, and where the woods and orchards
used to be, it looked just like a stubblefield, with the
stumps. After a while they had to make Christmas trees
out of rags, and stuff them with bran, like old-fashioned
dolls; but there were plenty of rags, because people got
so poor, buying presents for one another, that they
couldn't get any new clothes; and they just wore their
old ones to tatters. They got so poor that everybody had
to go to the poorhouse, except the confectioners, and the
fancy storekeepers, and the picture-booksellers, and the
expressmen; and *they* all got so rich and proud that they
would hardly wait upon a person when he came to buy;
it was perfectly shameful!

Well, after it had gone on about three or four months,
the little girl, whenever she came into the room in the
morning and saw those great ugly lumpy stockings dangling at the fireplace, and the disgusting presents around
everywhere, used to just sit down and burst out crying.
In six months she was perfectly exhausted; she couldn't
even cry any more; she just lay on the lounge and rolled
her eyes and panted. About the beginning of October
she took to sitting down on dolls, wherever she found
them—French dolls, or any kind—she hated the sight of
them so; and by Thanksgiving she was crazy, and just
slammed her presents across the room.

33

By that time people didn't carry presents around nicely any more. They flung them over the fence, or through the window, or anything; and, instead of running their tongues out and taking great pains to write For dear Papa, or Mamma, or Brother, or Sister, or Susie, or Sammie, or Billie, or Bobby, or Jimmie, or Jennie, or whoever it was, and troubling to get the spelling right, and then signing their names, and Xmas, 1888—, they used to write in the gift books, Take it, you horrid old thing! and then go and bang it against the front door. Nearly everybody had built barns to hold their presents, but pretty soon the barns overflowed, and then they used to let them lie out in the rain, or anywhere. Sometimes the police used to come and tell them to shovel their presents off the sidewalk, or they would arrest them.

"I thought you said everybody had gone to the poorhouse," interrupted the little girl.

"They did go, at first," said her papa; "but after a while the poorhouses got so full that they had to send the people back to their own houses. They tried to cry, when they got back, but they couldn't make the least sound."

"Why couldn't they?"

"Because they had lost their voices, saying 'Merry Christmas' so much. Did I tell you how it was on the Fourth of July?"

"No; how was it?" And the little girl nestled closer, in expectation of something uncommon.

Well, the night before, the boys stayed up to celebrate, as they always do, and fell asleep before twelve o'clock, as usual, expecting to be wakened by the bells and cannon. But it was nearly eight o'clock before the first boy in the United States woke up, and then he found out what the trouble was. As soon as he could get his clothes on, he ran out of the house and smashed a big cannon-torpedo down on the pavement; but it didn't make any more noise than a damp wad of paper, and, after he tried about twenty or thirty more, he began to pick them up and look at them. Every single torpedo was a big raisin! Then he just streaked it upstairs, and examined his firecrackers and toy pistol and two-dollar collection of fireworks, and found that they were nothing but sugar and candy painted up to look like fireworks! Before ten o'clock, every boy in the United States found out that his Fourth of July things had turned into Christmas things; and then they just sat down and cried—they were so mad. There are about twenty million boys in the United States, and so you can imagine what a noise they made. Some men got together before night, with a little powder that hadn't turned into purple sugar yet, and they said they would fire off *one* cannon, anyway. But the cannon burst into a thousand pieces, for it was nothing but rock candy, and some of the men nearly got killed. The Fourth of July orations all turned into

Christmas carols, and when anybody tried to read the Declaration, instead of saying, "When in the course of human events it becomes necessary," he was sure to sing "God rest you, merry gentlemen." It was perfectly awful.

The little girl drew a deep sigh of satisfaction. "And how was it at Thanksgiving?" she asked.

Her papa hesitated. "Well, I'm almost afraid to tell you. I'm afraid you'll think it's wicked."

"Well, tell, anyway," said the little girl.

Well, before it came Thanksgiving, it had leaked out who had caused all these Christmases. The little girl had suffered so much that she had talked about it in her sleep; and after that, hardly anybody would play with her. People just perfectly despised her, because if it had not been for her greediness, it wouldn't have happened; and now, when it came Thanksgiving, and she wanted them to go to church, and have squash, pie and turkey, and show their gratitude, they said that all the turkeys had been eaten up for her old Christmas dinners, and if she would stop the Christmases, they would see about the gratitude. Wasn't it dreadful? And the very next day the little girl began to send letters to the Christmas Fairy, and then telegrams, to stop it. But it didn't do any good; and then she got to calling at the Fairy's house, but the girl that came to the door always said "Not at home," or "Engaged," or "At dinner," or something like that; and so it went on till it came to the old one-a-year Christmas Eve. The little girl fell asleep, and when she woke up in the morning—

"She found it was all nothing but a dream," suggested the little girl.

"No, indeed!" said her papa. "It was all every bit true!"

"Well, what *did* she find out then?"

"Why, that it wasn't Christmas at last, and wasn't ever going to be, any more. Now it's time for breakfast."

The little girl held her papa fast around the neck. "You sha'n't go if you're going to leave it *so!*"

"How do you want it left?"

"Christmas once a year."

"All right," said her papa; and he went on again.

Well, there was the greatest rejoicing all over the country, and it extended clear up into Canada. The people met together everywhere, and kissed and cried for joy. The city carts went around and gathered up all the candy and raisins and nuts, and dumped them into the river; and it made the fish perfectly sick; and the whole United States, as far out as Alaska, was one blaze of bonfires, where the children were burning up their gift books and presents of all kinds. They had the greatest *time!*

The little girl went to thank the old Fairy because she had stopped its being Christmas, and she said she hoped she would keep her promise, and see that Christmas never, never came again. Then the Fairy frowned, and asked her if she was sure she knew what she meant; and the little girl asked her, why not? and the old Fairy said that now she was behaving just as greedily as ever, and she'd better look out. This made the little girl think it all over carefully again, and she said she would be willing to have it Christmas about once in a thousand years; and then she said a hundred, and then she said ten, and at last she got down to one. Then the Fairy said that was the good old way that had pleased people ever since Christmas began, and she was agreed. Then the little girl said, "What're your shoes made of?" And the Fairy said, "Leather." And the little girl said, "Bargain's done forever," and skipped off, and hippity-hopped the whole way home, she was so glad.

"How will that do?" asked the papa.

"First-rate!" said the little girl; but she hated to have the story stop, and was rather sober. However, her mamma put her head in at the door, and asked her papa:

"Are you never coming to breakfast? What have you been telling that child?"

"Oh, just a moral tale."

The little girl caught him around the neck again. "We know! Don't you tell *what*, Papa! Don't you tell *what!*"

Ashes of the Christmas Tree

By Yetza Gillespie

When Christmas trees at last are burned
Upon the hearth, they leap and flash
More brilliantly than other wood,
And wear a difference in the ash.

They do not lie in pallid gray,
But rise above the flames—oh, see!
They lift like clouds of silver moths,
For they have been the Christmas tree.

The Fir Tree

Retold from
Hans Christian Andersen

Once upon a time there was a pretty, green little
Fir Tree. The sun shone on him; he had plenty of fresh
air; and around him grew many large comrades, pines as
well as firs. But the little Fir was not satisfied. He did
not think of the sun and the fresh air. He wanted to be
a big tree like the others.

Sometimes the little children living in the cottages
nearby came into the woods looking for wild strawber-
ries. They ran about, laughing and talking, and often they
brought a whole pitcher full of berries, or a long row of
them threaded on a straw, and sat down near the young
Tree. "Oh, what a nice little Fir!" they said. But the Tree
did not like to hear them talk this way. He did not like
to be called "little."

By the time he was a year old he had grown a good
deal. Another year passed and he was another long bit

taller. With a fir tree one can tell by the number of shoots it has how old it is. "Oh, if I were only as tall as the other trees," he thought. "Then I could spread out my branches and look out into the wide world. The birds would build nests in my branches; and when there was a breeze I could bend with a stately bow like the others."

The Tree sighed, taking no pleasure in the sunbeams and the birds and the red clouds, which morning and evening, sailed above him.

In the wintertime, when the snow lay white and glittering on the ground, a hare would often come leaping along. Sometimes he jumped over the little Tree, and that made him very angry. But by the third winter the Tree had grown so large the hare had to go around it. That made the Tree feel better. "The most delightful thing in the world," he thought, "is to grow and grow and be tall and old."

In autumn the woodcutters came and cut down some of the largest trees. This happened every year and the little Fir Tree, which was not so little any more, was frightened. How he trembled as the magnificent trees fell to the earth with a great noise and crackling. After the branches had been lopped off, the trees looked so long and bare that it was hard to recognize them. Then they were laid in carts, and the horses dragged them out of the woods.

"What becomes of them?" the Fir Tree wondered.

In spring, when the Swallows and the Storks came,

the Tree said to them, "Do you know where they have been taken?"

The Swallows did not know anything about it, but one of the Storks nodded his head thoughtfully. "I think I know," he said. "As I was flying hither from Egypt, I met many ships with tall masts and they smelt of fir. You may feel proud of them, so majestic did they look."

"If I were only old enough to fly across the ocean!" sighed the Tree. "How does the ocean look? What is it like?"

"That would take a long time to explain," said the Stork, and off he flew.

"Rejoice in thy youth!" said the Sunbeams. "Rejoice

in thy growth!" And the Wind kissed the Tree, the Dew wept tears over him; but the Fir did not understand.

When Christmas came, many young trees were cut down. Some of them were neither so large nor so old as the Fir Tree, but they were always the finest looking. Their branches were left on them when they were laid carefully on the carts, and the horses drew them out of the woods.

"They are no taller than I," complained the Fir Tree. "Indeed one of them was much shorter. Why are they allowed to keep all their branches? Where are they going?"

"We know! We know!" twittered the Sparrows. "We have peeped in at the windows in the town below! We saw the trees planted in the middle of the warm rooms and ornamented with the most splendid things—with gilded apples, with gingerbread, with toys and hundreds of lights!"

A tremor ran through the Fir Tree. "And then? What happens after that?"

"We did not see anything more, but it was very beautiful."

"Ah, perhaps I shall know the same brightness some day," the Tree rejoiced. "That would be better than to cross the ocean. If Christmas would only come! I am as tall as the trees that were carried off last year. My branches spread as far. Oh, if I were only on the cart now! If I were only in the warm room with all the splendor and magnificence! Something better, something still

44

grander, is sure to follow—but what? How I long, how I suffer! I wonder what is the matter with me!"

"Rejoice in us!" said the Air and the Sunlight. "Rejoice in thy own youth!"

But the Tree did not rejoice. He grew and grew. He was green both winter and summer. "What a fine tree!" people said, and toward Christmas he was one of the first to be cut down. The ax struck deep, and the Tree fell to earth with a sigh. He was not happy; he could only think how sad it was to be taken away from the place where he had sprung up. He knew that never again would he see his dear old comrades, the little bushes and flowers around him; perhaps he would never even see the birds again. And he didn't like it at all.

The Tree was laid on a cart with several others and taken away. When he came to himself again he was being unloaded in a big yard, and two servants in handsome livery carried him into a large and beautiful drawing room. Here there were portraits hanging on the walls and, near the white porcelain stove, two big Chinese vases with lions on the covers. There were big easy chairs, silken cushions and tables filled with picture-books and toys. The Fir Tree was stuck upright in a tub filled with sand; but it did not look like a tub, for green cloth was hung all around it and it stood on a large, bright carpet.

A tremor ran through the Tree. What was going to happen? Several young ladies decorated it, aided by the servants. On one branch they hung little nets made of colored paper and filled with sugar plums. On the other boughs they hung gilded apples and walnuts which looked as though they had grown there. Then little blue and white and red candles were fastened to the branches. Among the foliage there were dolls which looked like people—the Tree had never seen anything like them before—and at the very top there was a large star of gold tinsel. It was really splendid—too splendid for any words to describe.

"Just wait till evening!" everybody said. "How the Tree will shine this evening!"

"Oh, if evening would only come!" thought the Tree. "If the candles were only lighted! What will happen then, I wonder. Will the other trees from the forest come to look at me? Will the sparrows beat against the windowpanes? Perhaps I shall take root and stand here winter and summer covered with ornaments!" He grew so impatient that he got a pain in his bark, and this with trees is the same as a headache with us.

When at last the candles were lighted, there was such brightness, such splendor, the Tree trembled in every bough. One of the candles set fire to the foliage, and it blazed up splendidly.

"Help! Help!" cried the young ladies and rushed to put out the fire.

After that the Tree did not dare tremble. He was quite bewildered by the glare and the brightness. Suddenly both the folding doors opened, and in rushed the children, with the older persons following more quietly. The

little ones stood quite still, but only for a moment. Then they shouted for joy, and the room echoed with their shouts. They began dancing around the Tree, pulling off one present after another.

"What are they doing?" thought the Tree. "What is to happen now?"

The candles burned down to the very branches, and as they burned down they were put out, one after another. Then the children were given permission to plunder the Tree, and they rushed upon it so violently that all its branches cracked. Then the children went on playing with their beautiful toys. No one even looked at the Tree, except the old nurse, who peeped in among the branches to see if there was a fig or an apple that had been overlooked.

"A story! A story!" the children cried, dragging a little fat man over toward the Tree. He sat down under it and said, "Now the Tree can listen, too. I shall tell you only one story, so which will you have: the one about Ivedy-Avedy, or the one about Klumpy-Dumpy who fell downstairs and yet married the princess and came to the throne after all?"

"Ivedy-Avedy!" cried some. "Klumpy-Dumpy!" cried others. There was a great deal of squealing, and finally the man told about Klumpy-Dumpy and the children clapped their hands and cried, "Go on! Go on!" The Fir Tree stood quite still, thinking: "Who knows? Perhaps I shall fall downstairs, too, and marry a princess!" And he looked forward to the next day, when he hoped to be decked out again with lights and toys and bright tinsel.

"I won't tremble tomorrow," he thought. "Tomorrow I shall hear again the story of Klumpy-Dumpy and perhaps that of Ivedy-Avedy, too." And all night long the Tree stood quite still, thinking.

The next morning in came the servants.

"Ah, now the splendor will begin again!" thought the Fir.

But no. The servants dragged him out of the room, up the stairs into the attic and there, in a dark corner, they left him. "What can this mean?" wondered the Tree, and he leaned against the wall lost in thought. And he had plenty of time for thinking. Days and nights passed and nobody came near him. When at last somebody did come up to the attic, it was only to leave some trunks.

48

There stood the Tree quite hidden. There stood the Tree quite forgotten.

"It is winter out-of-doors!" he thought. "The earth is hard and covered with snow. I could not be planted now. These people are really very kind. They have put me up here under shelter until spring comes! If only it were not so dark and lonely here! Not even a hare! I liked it out in the woods when the snow was on the ground and the hare leaped by; yes, even when he jumped over me. Ah, but I did not like it then."

"Squeak, squeak!" said a little Mouse, peeping out of his hole. Then another little Mouse came and they sniffed at the Fir Tree and ran in and out among the branches.

"It is dreadfully cold," said the Mouse. "Except for that, it would be nice here, wouldn't it, old Fir?"

"I am not old," said the Fir Tree. "There is many a tree much older than I."

"Where do you come from?" asked the Mice. "Tell us about the most beautiful place in the world. Have you ever been there? Have you ever been in the larder where there are cheeses lying on the shelves and hams hanging from the ceiling, where one may dance on tallow candles; a place where one goes in lean and comes out fat?"

"I know of no such place," said the Tree. "But I know the woods where the sun shines and the birds sing." Then he told of the time when he was young, and the little Mice had never heard the like before.

"How much you have seen!" they said. "How happy you must have been!"

"I?" said the Fir Tree, thinking it over. "Yes, those really were happy times." Then he told about Christmas Eve, when he had been decked out with beautiful ornaments and candles.

"Oh," said the little Mice. "How lucky you have been, old Fir Tree."

"I am not old," said he. "I came from the woods only this winter."

"But what wonderful stories you know!" said the Mice, and the next night they came with four other little Mice who wanted to hear the stories also. The more the Fir Tree talked about his youth, the more plainly he remembered it himself, and he realized that those times had really been very happy times. "But they may come again. Klumpy-Dumpy fell downstairs and yet he married a princess," said the Fir Tree. And at that moment he remembered a little birch tree growing out in the woods. To the Fir she seemed like a princess.

"Who is Klumpy-Dumpy?" asked the Mice. So the Fir Tree told the story, and the little Mice were so pleased they jumped to the very top of the Tree. The next night two more Mice came, and on Sunday two Rats. But they said the stories were not interesting. This worried the little Mice. They began to think the stories not very interesting either.

"Is that the only story you know?" asked the Rats.

"Only that one," said the Tree. "I heard it on the happiest night of my life; only then I did not know how happy I was."

"It's a silly story. Don't you know one about bacon-and-tallow candles? Can't you tell any larder stories?"

"No," said the Tree.

"Then good-by," said the Rats and went home.

At last the little Mice stopped coming, and the Tree sighed. "After all I liked having the sleek little Mice listen to my stories, but that is over now. When I am brought out again I am going to enjoy myself."

But when was that to be? Why, one morning a number of people came up to the attic. Trunks were moved and the Tree was pulled out and thrown down on the floor. Then a man drew him toward the stairs, where the sun shone.

"Now life begins again," thought the Tree. He felt the fresh air, the first sunbeam—and then he was out in the yard. Everything happened so quickly he quite forgot to look to himself. The yard was right next to a garden where fragrant roses hung over the fence and lindens were in bloom. The Swallows flew by and said, "Quirre-vit! My husband is come!" But it was not the Fir Tree that they meant.

"Now I shall enjoy life," said he joyfully, and spread out his branches. But alas, they were all withered and yellow. He lay in a corner among weeds and nettles. The golden tinsel star was still on the tree, and it glittered in the sunlight.

In the yard some children were playing—the same children who had danced around the Fir Tree at Christmas time. They were glad to see him again, and the youngest child ran up and tore off the golden star.

"Look what is still on the ugly old Christmas Tree!" said he. And he trampled on the branches, so that they cracked beneath his feet.

The tree looked at the beautiful garden and then at himself. He wished he had stayed in his dark corner in the loft. He thought of his youth in the woods, of the merry Christmas Eve, and of the little Mice who had listened so eagerly to the story of Klumpy-Dumpy.

" 'Tis over," said the poor Tree. "Had I but been happy when I had reason to be! But 'tis all over now."

Then the gardener's boy chopped the Tree into small pieces, and the wood flamed up splendidly under a large brewing kettle. It sighed deeply, and each sigh was like a shot.

The children went on playing in the yard. On his chest the youngest wore the gold star which the Tree had had on the happiest evening of his life. But that was over now—the Tree gone, the story finished. Everything was over; every tale must come to an end at last.

PRESENTS

By Marchette Chute

I wanted a rifle for Christmas,
  I wanted a bat and a ball,
I wanted some skates and a bicycle,
  But I didn't want mittens at all.

I wanted a whistle
  And I wanted a kite,
I wanted a pocketknife
  That shut up tight.
I wanted some boots
  And I wanted a kit,
But I didn't want mittens one little bit.

I told them I didn't like mittens,
  I told them as plain as plain.
I told them I didn't WANT mittens,
  And they've given me mittens again!

A Miserable, Merry Christmas

A Real Adventure in California in the Seventies

By Lincoln Steffens

What interested me in our new neighborhood was not the school, nor the room I was to have in the house all to myself, but the stable which was built back of the house. My father let me direct the making of a stall, a little smaller than the other stalls, for my pony, and I prayed and hoped and my sister Lou believed that that meant that I would get the pony, perhaps for Christmas. I pointed out to her that there were three other stalls and no horses at all. This I said in order that she should answer it. She could not. My father, sounded, said that some day we might have horses and a cow; meanwhile the stable added to the value of a house. "Some day" is a pain to a boy who lives in and knows only "now."

My good little sisters, to comfort me, remarked that

"A Miserable Merry Christmas" is a chapter about Lincoln Steffens' boyhood from his autobiography, *Boy on Horseback.*

Christmas was coming, but Christmas was always coming and grownups were always talking about it, asking you what you wanted and then giving you what they wanted you to have. Though everybody knew what I wanted, I told them all again. My mother knew that I told God, too, every night. I wanted a pony, and to make sure that they understood, I declared that I wanted nothing else.

"Nothing but a pony?" my father asked.

"Nothing," I said.

"Not even a pair of high boots?"

That was hard. I did want boots, but I stuck to the pony. "No, not even boots."

"Nor candy? There ought to be something to fill your stocking with, and Santa Claus can't put a pony into a stocking."

That was true, and he couldn't lead a pony down the chimney either. But no. "All I want is a pony," I said. "If I can't have a pony, give me nothing, nothing."

Now I had been looking myself for the pony I wanted, going to sales stables, inquiring of horsemen, and I had seen several that would do. My father let me "try" them. I tried so many ponies that I was learning fast to sit a horse. I chose several, but my father always found some fault with them. I was in despair. When Christmas was at hand, I had given up all hope of a pony, and on Christmas Eve I hung up my stocking along with my sisters', of whom, by the way, I now had three. I haven't mentioned them or their coming because, you under-

stand, they were girls, and girls, young girls, counted
for nothing in my manly life. They did not mind me
either; they were so happy that Christmas Eve that I
caught some of their merriment. I speculated on what
I'd get; I hung up the biggest stocking I had, and we all
went reluctantly to bed to wait till morning. Not to
sleep; not right away. We were told that we must not
only sleep promptly, we must not wake up till seven-
thirty the next morning—or if we did, we must not go
to the fireplace for our Christmas. Impossible.

We did sleep that night, but we woke up at six A.M.
We lay in our beds and debated through the open doors
whether to obey till say, half past six. Then we bolted. I
don't know who started it, but there was a rush. We all
disobeyed; we raced to disobey and get first to the fireplace in the front room downstairs. And there they were,
the gifts, all sorts of wonderful things, mixed-up piles
of presents; only, as I disentangled the mess, I saw that
my stocking was empty; it hung limp; not a thing in it;
and under and around it—nothing. My sisters had knelt
down each by her pile of gifts; they were squealing with
delight, till they looked up and saw me standing there in
my nightgown with nothing. They left their piles to
come to me and look with me at my empty place. Nothing. They felt my stocking: nothing.

I don't remember whether I cried at that moment, but
my sisters did. They ran with me back to my bed, and
there we all cried till I became indignant. That helped
some. I got up, dressed, and driving my sisters away, I

went alone out into the yard, down to the stable, and there, all by myself, I wept. My mother came out to me by and by; she found me in my pony stall, sobbing on the floor, and she tried to comfort me. But I heard my father outside; he had come part way with her, and she was having some sort of angry quarrel with him. She tried to comfort me; besought me to come to breakfast. I could not; I wanted no comfort and no breakfast. She left me and went on into the house with sharp words for my father.

I don't know what kind of breakfast the family had. My sisters said it was "awful." They were ashamed to enjoy their own toys. They came to me, and I was rude. I ran away from them. I went around to the front of the house, sat down on the steps, and, the crying over, I ached. I was wronged, I was hurt—I can feel now what I felt like, and I am sure that if one could see the wounds upon our hearts, there would be found still upon mine a scar from that terrible Christmas morning. And my father, the practical joker, he must have been hurt, too, a little. I saw him looking out of the window. He was watching me or something for an hour or two, drawing back the curtain ever so little lest I catch him, but I saw his face, and I think I can see now the anxiety upon it, the worried impatience.

After—I don't know how long—surely an hour or two, I was brought to the climax of my agony by the sight of a man riding a pony down the street, a pony and a brand-new saddle; the most beautiful saddle I ever saw,

and it was a boy's saddle; the man's feet were not in the
stirrups; his legs were too long. The outfit was perfect; it
was the realization of all my dreams, the answer to all
my prayers. A fine new bridle, with a light curb bit. And
the pony! As he drew near, I saw that the pony was
really a small horse, what we called an Indian pony, a
bay, with black mane and tail, and one white foot and a
white star on his forehead. For such a horse as that I
would have given, I could have forgiven anything.

But the man, a disheveled fellow with a blackened
eye and a fresh-cut face, came along, reading the num-
bers on the houses, and as my hopes—my impossible
hopes—rose, he looked at our door and passed by, he
and the pony, and the saddle and the bridle. Too much.
I fell upon the steps, and having wept before, I broke
now into such a flood of tears that I was a floating wreck
when I heard a voice.

"Say, kid," it said, "do you know a boy named Lennie
Steffens?"

I looked up. It was the man on the pony, back again,
at our horse block.

"Yes," I spluttered through my tears. "That's me."

"Well," he said, "then this is your horse. I've been
looking all over for you and your house. Why don't you
put your number where it can be seen?"

"Get down," I said.

He got down, and he boosted me up to the saddle. He
offered to fit the stirrups to me, but I didn't want him to.
I wanted to ride.

A *Miserable, Merry* Christmas

"What's the matter with you?" he said, angrily. "What you crying for? Don't you like the horse? He's a dandy, this horse. I know him of old. He's fine at cattle; he'll drive 'em alone."

I hardly heard, I could scarcely wait, but he persisted. He adjusted the stirrups, and then, finally, off I rode, slowly, at a walk, so happy, so thrilled, that I did not know what I was doing. I did not look back at the house or the man, I rode off up the street, taking note of everything—of the reins, of the pony's long mane, of the carved leather saddle. I had never seen anything so beautiful. And mine! I was going to ride up past Miss Kay's house. But I noticed on the horn of the saddle some stains like raindrops, so I turned and trotted home, not to the house but to the stable. There was the family, father, mother, sisters, all working for me, all happy. They had been putting in place the tools of my new business: blankets, currycomb, brush, pitchfork—everything, and there was hay in the loft.

"What did you come back so soon for?" somebody asked. "Why didn't you go on riding?"

I pointed to the stains. "I wasn't going to get my new saddle rained on," I said. And my father laughed. "It isn't raining," he said. "Those are not raindrops."

"They are tears," my mother gasped, and she gave my father a look which sent him off to the house. Worse still, my mother offered to wipe away the tears still running out of my eyes. I gave her such a look as she had

61

given him, and she went off after my father, drying her own tears.

My sisters remained and we all unsaddled the pony, put on his halter, led him to his stall, tied and fed him.

It began really to rain; so all the rest of that memorable day we curried and combed that pony. The girls plaited his mane, forelock, and tail, while I pitchforked hay to him and curried and brushed, curried and brushed. For a change we brought him out to drink; we led him up and down, blanketed like a race horse; we took turns at that. But the best, the most inexhaustible fun, was to clean him.

When we went reluctantly to our midday Christmas dinner, we smelt of horse, and my sisters had to wash their faces and hands. I was asked to, but I wouldn't till my mother bade me look in the mirror. Then I washed up—quick. My face was caked with muddy lines of tears that had coursed over my cheeks to my mouth. Having washed away that shame, I ate my dinner, and as I ate I grew hungrier and hungrier. It was my first meal that day, and as I filled up on the turkey and the stuffing, the cranberries and the pies, the fruit and the nuts—as I swelled, I could laugh. My mother said I still choked and sobbed now and then, but I laughed, too; I saw and enjoyed my sisters' presents till—I had to go out and attend to my pony, who was there, really and truly there, the promise, the beginning, of a happy double life. And —I went and looked to make sure—there was the saddle, too, and the bridle.

But that Christmas, which my father had planned so carefully, was it the best or the worst I ever knew? He often asked me that; I never could answer as a boy. I think now that it was both. It covered the whole distance from brokenhearted misery to bursting happiness —too fast. A grownup could hardly have stood it.

THE BELLS

By Edgar Allan Poe

Hear the sledges with the bells—
  Silver bells!
What a world of merriment their melody foretells!
  How they tinkle, tinkle, tinkle,
    In the icy air of night!
  While the stars that oversprinkle
  All the heavens seem to twinkle
    With a crystalline delight;
  Keeping time, time, time,
    In a sort of Runic rhyme,
To the tintinnabulation that so musically wells
  From the bells, bells, bells, bells,
    Bells, bells, bells—
From the jingling and the tinkling of the bells.

Yuletide Customs in Many Lands

By Lou Crandall

Christmas in May? It sounds strange, doesn't it? And yet in the early centuries of Christianity, the birthday of Jesus probably was sometimes celebrated in May, sometimes in other months; certainly it was often observed in January. This was because the exact date of the birth of Christ has never been known.

It was in the fourth century that December twenty-fifth was named by Church authorities as the date of the Nativity. And during the next hundred years the celebration of this event on the day we now call Christmas became a custom generally accepted throughout the Christian world. The reason why December twenty-fifth was selected is another mystery. Possibly it was because that was the time when the winter solstice was celebrated in ancient Rome. At any rate, the choice of the twenty-fifth day of December accounts for many of our Christmas customs, for it fell within the time of the

65

big winter festivals and feasts, not only of Rome but also of the pagans in the north.

And now let us see how today, and in other countries than our own, Christmas time is observed.

England is a country where the celebration is a great deal like ours. Christmas Eve the tree is decorated, and stockings are hung in anticipation of a visit from Santa Claus or Father Christmas. Perhaps during the evening a group of singers called "waits" will serenade the household. On Christmas Day there will be gifts and church and a tremendous noontime dinner with roast beef, or goose, and plum pudding.

Possibly the most-loved custom of an English Christmas is that of burning the Yule log—an immense block of wood that fills the fireplace. The Yule log is one of the Christmas customs that has come to us from pagan times when the druids kept sacred fires burning. In the Middle Ages the log was very large. It was carefully chosen long beforehand and it was dragged into the great hall in the midst of much celebration. It was the custom, too, to light the log with a piece of one left over from the year before.

Now let's travel farther north and see what is going on in two of the Scandinavian countries. Swedish children have their gifts and tree on Christmas Eve, and the big Christmas dinner is that night also. Sometimes exciting gifts are thrown in the front doors by mysterious donors who run away before anyone can find out who they are. Christmas Day itself, the whole family rises extremely early and goes to church.

In Norway also there is a Christmas tree and a grand feast. The gifts are often hidden away in different parts of the house for the children to find. In both of these northern countries sheaves of grain are put on top of the houses or barns or are hung on poles in the yards, that the birds, too, may enjoy a Christmas dinner.

The great gift of Germany to the customs of Christmas is the decorated tree—for many years the heart of German Christmas celebrations. Probably in early times, pagans honored trees during some of their festivities, but it is likely they were not used in connection with Christ-

mas until the sixteenth century. It was Martin Luther, so many people believe, who thought of decorating the first Christmas tree, inspired by watching the beauty of brilliant stars against a dark sky one Christmas Eve.

In Holland and Belgium, Christmas time itself is celebrated mostly by church services. But there is another day the children love; this is the sixth of December, the feast day of St. Nicholas. It is said that during the evening of December fifth, St. Nicholas, dressed in magnificent robes, comes riding on a horse, and goes about inquiring as to the behavior of the children. If the report is satisfactory, in the morning they will find their shoes full of gifts; but if the children are naughty, they are liable to find instead rods of birch!

In France, for grownups, the day of feasting and visiting is New Year's. Christmas is for the most part a church celebration. But the children are not forgotten at Noël, or Christmas time. Christmas Eve they leave their shoes by the chimney, and in the morning they find them full of presents, which they believe have been left for them by the Christ Child, le petit Jésus. The end of the Christmas season also brings excitement in the form of a special Twelfth Night cake within which has been baked some little token such as a bean or china figure. Whoever gets the piece of cake containing the token becomes "king" or "queen" for the rest of the party.

As we travel farther south to Italy, we find that here, too, Christmas is mostly a religious occasion. For twenty-four hours before Christmas Eve a strict fast is kept.

Then on Christmas Eve a splendid banquet is held, and after it comes the exciting drawing of presents from the Urn of Fate. The Urn is a big crock filled with gifts. These are drawn out, and as sometimes the presents are blanks, there is much excitement and occasionally disappointment among the children. But eventually there is a gift for everyone, so all are happy. Now comes the Christmas Eve services in the church. As the families go through the crowded streets, they find them very gay. The streets are bright with bonfires and fireworks, and some of the people are carrying torches.

On Epiphany, which comes on the sixth of January, the Italian children have another treat in store for them. On the Eve of Epiphany, or Twelfth Night, the children hang up their stockings and during the night a little old lady, Befana, is believed to come and leave delightful gifts in the stockings of the good children, but only birch rods or charcoal ashes in those of the bad.

Wouldn't it seem strange to celebrate Christmas in the summertime? And yet that is exactly what happens in Australia, where December twenty-fifth occurs during their summer. So, strangely enough, a picnic is often an important part of Christmas Day festivities there.

All the unusual Christmas observances are not in far-away lands, by any means. Right here on our own continent, in Mexico, Christmas is celebrated with a number of interesting customs. Possibly the one the children enjoy most is the breaking of the *pinata*. A pinata is a bowl, gaily decorated and filled with little toys and candies and hung up above the heads of the children. The children in turn are blindfolded and given a stick; each has a chance to break the pinata. This is not easy to do when one is blindfolded, and many fail. But at last one child will break it—and then what fun—for everyone rushes to gather up some of the goodies and toys.

In Mexico the gift day for children is not Christmas, but Epiphany. The night before, the children place their shoes in the window or at the foot of their beds. Then the next morning, there the shoes are, brimful of presents—gifts, they say, from the Magi on their way to see the Christ Child.

Lord Octopus Went To The Christmas Fair

By Stella Mead

Lord Octopus went to the Christmas Fair;
An hour and a half he was traveling there.
  Then he had to climb
  For a weary time
  To the slimy block
  Of a sandstone rock,
  And creep, creep away
  To the big wide bay
  Where a stout old whale
  Held his Christmas Sale.

Lord Octopus went to the Christmas Fair;
An hour and a half he was traveling there.
His two little girls and two little boys
Were waiting at home for their Christmas toys;
  And dear old Granny,
  And fat Aunt Fanny,
  And Cousin Dolly,
  And Sister Molly
Would think Lord Octopus quite unpleasant
Unless he brought them a Christmas present.

71

Lord Octopus Went to the Christmas Fair

Lord Octopus went to the Christmas Fair;
An hour and a half he was traveling there.
He purchased two hoops for the little boys.
He purchased two rings for the girls, as toys.
  He bought for Granny
  A sweet nightcap,
  To please Aunt Fanny
  A game of snap;
  For Cousin Dolly
  A winter wrap,
  For Sister Molly
  A sea-route map.

With hoops for the boys, for the girls round rings,
The wrap, and the rest of the Christmas things,
Tied up into parcels and packets strong,
Lord Octopus merrily went along.
On every arm he hung a present,
And said, "It's really rather pleasant
To have eight arms instead of two.
What can those human creatures do
With just two arms for all the toys
They have to buy their girls and boys?"

CHRISTMAS TREE

By Aileen Fisher

I'll find me a spruce
in the cold white wood
with wide green boughs
and a snowy hood.

I'll pin on a star
with five gold spurs
to mark my spruce
from the pines and firs.

I'll make me a score
of suet balls
to tie to my spruce
when the cold dusk falls,

And I'll hear next day
from the sheltering trees,
the Christmas carols
of the chickadees.

Silent Night, Holy Night

*(This carol was first sung in a little church in Austria almost
150 years ago. It was composed by the organist one Christmas
Eve. And it was sung the next day to the strumming of a guitar
because the organ had broken down!)*

Silent night! Holy night!
All is calm, all is bright,
Round yon Virgin Mother and Child,
Holy Infant so tender and mild,
Sleep in heavenly peace,
Sleep in heavenly peace.

Deck the Halls

*(This old song was first sung in Wales when Christmas merry-
making lasted only as long as the great yule log burned.)*

Deck the halls with boughs of holly,
Fa la la la la, la la la la.
'Tis the season to be jolly,
Fa la la la la, la la la la.
Don we now our gay apparel,
Fa la la, la la la, la la la.
Troll the ancient Christmas carol, ·
Fa la la la la, la la la la.

Fast away the old year passes,
Fa la la la la, la la la la.
Hail the new! ye lads and lasses,
Fa la la la la, la la la la.
Sing we joyous all together,
Fa la la, la la la, la la la.
Heedless of the wind and weather.
Fa la la la la, la la la la.

It Came Upon a Midnight Clear

(Edmund Sears, an American minister, wrote this carol as a poem in 1850. The poem was so lovely that a friend suggested the words be set to music. Dr. Sears sent his poem to Richard Willis in Boston who composed the beautiful melody.)

It came upon a midnight clear,
That glorious song of old,
From angels bending near the earth,
To touch their harps of gold;
"Peace on the earth, good will to men,
From heav'ns all gracious King";
The world in solemn stillness lay
To hear the angels sing.

O CHRISTMAS TREE

(The tune of this carol is said to be one of the oldest in the world. During the Civil War, it was used for the Confederate song, "Maryland, My Maryland.")

O Christmas Tree, O Christmas Tree,
Your branches green delight us!
O Christmas Tree, O Christmas Tree,
Your branches green delight us.
They're green when summer days are bright;
They're green when winter snow is white.
O Christmas Tree, O Christmas Tree,
Your branches green delight us.

FROM ENGLAND

WASSAIL SONG

(Wassail! So sang the merry carolers in old England as they went from house to house carrying their wassail bowl filled with hot, spiced ale.)

Here we come a-wassailing,
Among the leaves so green,
Here we come a-wandering,
So fair to be seen.

Love and joy come to you,
And to you your wassail too,
And God bless you, and send you a happy New Year,
And God send you a happy New Year.

THE BIRDS

(This lovely carol is hundreds of years old.)

From out of a wood did a cuckoo fly,
 Cuckoo,
He came to a manger with joyful cry,
 Cuckoo,
He hopped, he curtsied, round he flew,
And loud his jubilation grew,
 Cuckoo, Cuckoo, Cuckoo.

A pigeon flew over to Galilee,
    Vrercroo,
He strutted, and cooed, and was full of glee,
    Vrercroo,
And showed with jewelled wings unfurled
His joy that Christ was in the world,
    Vrercroo, Vrercroo, Vrercroo.

A dove settled down upon Nazareth,
    Tsucroo,
And tenderly chanted with all his breath,
    Tsucroo:
"O you," he cooed, "so good and true,
My beauty do I give to you —"
    Tsucroo, Tsucroo, Tsucroo.

SHEPHERDS, SHAKE OFF

Shepherds! shake off your drowsy sleep,
Rise and leave your silly sheep;
Angels from heav'n around loud singing
Tidings of great joy are bringing.

Hark! even now the bells ring round,
Listen to their merry sound;
Hark! how the birds new songs are making,
As if winter's chains were breaking.

Chorus:
Shepherds! the chorus come and swell!
Sing Noel, Oh, sing Noel.

YOUR DROWSY SLEEP

(This old carol came from the hillsides of France where shep-herds tend their sheep. It is so old no one knows who wrote the words or the melody.)

The Jar of Rosemary

By Maud Lindsay

There was once a little prince whose mother, the queen, was sick. All summer she lay in bed, and everything was kept quiet in the palace; but when the autumn came she grew better. Every day brought color to her cheeks, and strength to her limbs, and by and by the little prince was allowed to go into her room and stand beside her bed to talk to her.

He was very glad of this for he wanted to ask her what she would like for a Christmas present; and as soon as he had kissed her, and laid his cheek against hers, he whispered his question in her ear.

"What should I like for a Christmas present?" said the queen. "A smile and a kiss and a hug around the neck; these are the dearest gifts I know."

But the prince was not satisfied with this answer. "Smiles and kisses and hugs you can have every day," he said, "but think, Mother, think, if you could choose

84

the thing you wanted most in all the world what would you take?"

"If I might take my choice of all the world I believe a little jar of rosemary like that which bloomed in my mother's window when I was a little girl would please me better than anything else."

The little prince was delighted to hear this, and as soon as he had gone out of the queen's room he sent a servant to his father's greenhouses to inquire for a rosemary plant.

But the servant came back with disappointing news. There were carnation pinks in the king's greenhouses and roses with golden hearts, and lovely lilies; but there was no rosemary. Rosemary was a common herb and grew, mostly, in country gardens, so the king's gardeners said.

"Then go into the country for it," said the little prince. "No matter where it grows, my mother must have it for a Christmas present."

So messengers went into the country here, there, and everywhere to seek the plant, but each one came back with the same story to tell; there was rosemary, enough and to spare, in the spring, but the frost had been in the country and there was not a green sprig left to bring to the little prince for his mother's Christmas present.

Two days before Christmas, however, news was brought that rosemary had been found, a lovely green plant growing in a jar, right in the very city where the prince himself lived.

"But where is it?" said he. "Why have you not brought it with you? Go and get it at once."

"Well, as for that," said the servant who had found the plant, "there is a little difficulty. The old woman to whom the rosemary belongs did not want to sell it even though I offered her a handful of silver for it."

"Then give her a purse of gold," said the little prince.

So a purse filled so full of gold that it could not hold another piece was taken to the old woman; but presently it was brought back. She would not sell her rosemary; no, not even for a purse of gold.

"Perhaps if Your Little Highness would go yourself and ask her, she might change her mind," said the prince's nurse. So the royal carriage drawn by six white horses was brought, and the little prince and his servants rode away to the old woman's house, and when they got there, the first thing they spied was the little green plant in a jar standing in the old woman's window.

The old woman, herself, came to the door, and she was glad to see the little prince. She invited him in, and bade him warm his hands by the fire, and gave him a cooky from her cupboard to eat.

She had a little grandson no older than the prince, but he was sick and could not run about and play like other children. He lay in a little white bed in the old woman's room, and the little prince, after he had eaten the cooky, spoke to him, and took out his favorite plaything, which he always carried in his pocket, and showed it to him.

The prince's favorite plaything was a ball which was

like no other ball that had ever been made. It was woven of magic stuff as bright as the sunlight, as sparkling as the starlight, and as golden as the moon at harvest time. And when the little prince threw it into the air, or bounced it on the floor or turned it in his hands, it rang like a chime of silver bells.

The sick child laughed to hear it, and held out his hands for it, and the prince let him hold it, which pleased the grandmother as much as the child.

But pleased though she was, she would not sell the rosemary. She had brought it from the home where she had lived when her little grandson's father was a boy, she said, and she hoped to keep it till she died. So the prince and his servants had to go home without it.

No sooner had they gone than the sick child began to talk of the wonderful ball.

"If I had such a ball to hold in my hand," he said, "I should be contented all the day."

"You may as well wish for the moon in the sky," said his grandmother; but she thought of what he said, and in the evening when he was asleep she put her shawl around her, and taking the jar of rosemary with her she hastened to the king's palace.

When she got there the servants asked her errand but she would answer nothing till they had taken her to the little prince.

"Silver and gold would not buy the rosemary," she said when she saw him; "but if you will give me your golden ball for my little grandchild you may have the plant."

"But my ball is the most wonderful ball that was ever made!" cried the little prince; "and it is my favorite plaything. I would not give it away for anything."

And so the old woman had to go home with her jar of rosemary under her shawl.

The next day was the day before Christmas and there was a great stir and bustle in the palace. The queen's physician had said that she might sit up to see the Christmas Tree that night, and have her presents with the rest of the family; and everyone was running to and fro to get things in readiness for her.

The queen had so many presents, and very fine they were, too, that the Christmas Tree could not hold them all, so they were put on a table before the throne and wreathed around with holly and with pine. The little prince went in with his nurse to see them, and to put his gift, which was a jewel, among them.

"She wanted a jar of rosemary," he said as he looked at the glittering heap.

"She will never think of it again when she sees these things. You may be sure of that," said the nurse.

But the little prince was not sure. He thought of it himself many times that day, and once, when he was playing with his ball, he said to the nurse:

"If I had a rosemary plant I'd be willing to sell it for a purse full of gold. Wouldn't you?"

"Indeed, yes," said the nurse; "and so would anyone else in his right senses. You may be sure of that."

The little boy was not satisfied, though, and presently when he had put his ball up and stood at the window watching the snow which had come to whiten the earth for Christ's birthday, he said to the nurse:

"I wish it were spring. It is easy to get rosemary then, is it not?"

"Your Little Highness is like the king's parrot that knows but one word with your rosemary, rosemary, rosemary," said the nurse who was a little out of patience by that time. "Her Majesty, the Queen, only asked for it to please you. You may be sure of that."

But the little prince was not sure; and when the nurse had gone to her supper and he was left by chance for a moment alone, he put on his coat of fur, and taking the ball with him he slipped away from the palace, and hastened toward the old woman's house.

He had never been out at night by himself before, and he might have felt a little afraid had it not been for the friendly stars that twinkled in the sky above him.

"We will show you the way," they seemed to say; and he trudged on bravely in their light, till, by and by, he came to the house and knocked at the door.

Now the little sick child had been talking of the wonderful ball all the evening. "Did you see how it shone, Grandmother? And did you hear how the little bells rang?" he said; and it was just then that the little prince knocked at the door.

The old woman made haste to answer the knock and when she saw the prince she was too astonished to speak.

"Here is the ball," he cried, putting it into her hands. "Please give me the rosemary for my mother."

And so it happened that when the queen sat down before her great table of gifts the first thing she spied was a jar of sweet rosemary like that which had bloomed in her mother's window when she was a little girl.

"I should rather have it than all the other gifts in the world," she said; and she took the little prince in her arms and kissed him.

ONE NIGHT

By Marchette Chute

Last winter when the snow was deep
   And sparkled on the lawn
And there was moonlight everywhere,
   I saw a little fawn.

I watched her playing in the snow.
   She did not want to leave.
She must have known before she came
   That it was Christmas Eve.

Mr. Edwards Meets Santa Claus

By Laura Ingalls Wilder

The days were short and cold, the wind whistled sharply, but there was no snow. Cold rains were falling. Day after day the rain fell, pattering from the roof and pouring from the eaves.

Mary and Laura stayed close by the fire, sewing their nine patch-quilt blocks, or cutting paper dolls from scraps of wrapping paper, and hearing the wet sound of the rain. Every night was so cold that they expected to see snow the next morning, but in the morning they saw only sad, wet grass.

They pressed their noses against the squares of glass in the windows that Pa had made, and they were glad they could see out. But they wished they could see snow.

Laura was anxious because Christmas was near, and Santa Claus and his reindeer could not travel without

"Mr. Edwards Meets Santa Claus" is a chapter from the well-loved book, *The Little House on the Prairie* by Laura Ingalls Wilder.

snow. Mary was afraid that, even if it snowed, Santa Claus could not find them, so far away in Indian Territory.

When they asked Ma about this, she said she didn't know.

"What day is it?" they asked her, anxiously. "How many more days until Christmas?" And they counted off the days on their fingers, till there was only one more day left.

Rain was still falling that morning. There was not one crack in the gray sky. They felt almost sure there would be no Christmas. Still, they kept hoping.

Just before noon the light changed. The clouds broke and drifted apart, shining white in a clear blue sky. The sun shone, birds sang, and thousands of drops of water sparkled on the grasses. But when Ma opened the door to let in the fresh, cold air, they heard the creek roaring.

They had not thought about the creek. Now they knew they would have no Christmas, because Santa Claus could not cross that roaring creek.

Pa came in, bringing a fat turkey. If it weighed less than twenty pounds, he said, he'd eat it, feathers and all. He asked Laura, "How's that for a Christmas dinner? Think you can manage one of those drumsticks?"

She said, yes, she could. Then Mary asked him if the creek was going down, and he said it was still rising.

Ma said it was too bad. She hated to think of Mr. Edwards eating his bachelor cooking all alone on Christmas Day. Mr. Edwards had been asked to eat Christmas dinner with them, but Pa shook his head and said a man would risk his neck, trying to cross that creek now.

"No," he said. "That current's too strong. We'll just have to make up our minds that Edwards won't be here tomorrow."

Of course that meant that Santa Claus could not come, either.

Laura and Mary tried not to mind too much. They watched Ma dress the wild turkey, and it was a very fat turkey. They were lucky little girls to have a good house to live in, and a warm fire to sit by, and such a turkey for their Christmas dinner. Ma said so, and it was true. Ma

95

said it was too bad that Santa Claus couldn't come this year, but that they were such good girls that he hadn't forgotten them; he would surely come next year.

Still, they were not happy.

After supper that night they washed their hands and faces, buttoned their red flannel nightgowns, tied their nightcap strings, and soberly said their prayers. They lay down in bed and pulled the covers up. It did not seem at all like Christmas time.

Pa and Ma sat silent by the fire. After a while Ma asked why Pa didn't play the fiddle, and he said, "I don't seem to have the heart to, Caroline."

After a longer while, Ma suddenly stood up.

"I'm going to hang up your stockings, girls," she said. "Maybe something will happen."

Laura's heart jumped. But then she thought again of the creek and she knew nothing could happen.

Ma took one of Mary's clean stockings and one of Laura's, and she hung them from the mantel shelf, on either side of the fireplace. Laura and Mary watched her over the edge of their bed covers.

"Now go to sleep," Ma said, kissing them good night. "Morning will come quicker if you are asleep."

She sat down by the fire and Laura almost went to sleep. She woke up a little when she heard Pa say, "You've only made it worse, Caroline."

And she thought she heard Ma say: "No, Charles. There's the white sugar." But perhaps she was dreaming.

Then she heard Jack growl savagely. The door latch

96

rattled and someone said, "Ingalls! Ingalls!" Pa was stirring up the fire, and when he opened the door Laura saw that it was morning. The outdoors was gray.

"Great fishhooks, Edwards! Come in, man! What's happened?" he exclaimed.

Laura saw the stocking limply dangling, and she scrooged her shut eyes into the pillow. She heard Pa piling wood on the fire, and she heard Mr. Edwards say he had carried his clothes on his head when he swam the creek. His teeth rattled and his voice shivered. He would be all right, he said, when he got warm.

"It was too big a risk, Edwards," Pa said. "We're glad you're here but that was too big a risk for a Christmas dinner."

"Your little ones ought to have a Christmas," Mr. Edwards replied. "No creek could stop me, after I fetched them their gifts from Independence."

Laura sat straight up in bed. "Did you see Santa Claus?" she shouted.

"I sure did," Mr. Edwards said.

"Where? When? What did he look like? What did he say? Did he really give you something for us?" Mary and Laura cried.

"Wait, wait a minute!" Mr. Edwards laughed. And Ma said she would put the presents in the stockings, as Santa Claus intended. She said they mustn't look.

Mr. Edwards came and sat on the floor by their bed, and he answered every question they asked him. They honestly tried not to look at Ma, and they didn't quite see what she was doing.

When he saw the creek rising, Mr. Edwards said, he had known that Santa Claus could not get across it. ("But you crossed it," Laura said. "Yes," said Mr. Edwards, "but Santa Claus is too old and fat. He couldn't make it, where a long, lean razorback like me could do so.") And Mr. Edwards reasoned that if Santa Claus couldn't cross the creek, likely he would come no farther south than Independence. Why should he come forty miles across the prairie, only to be turned back? Of course he wouldn't do that!

So Mr. Edwards had walked to Independence. ("In the rain?" Mary asked. Mr. Edwards said he wore his rubber coat.) And there, coming down the street in Independence, he had met Santa Claus. ("In the daytime?" Laura asked. She hadn't thought that anyone could see Santa Claus in the daytime. No, Mr. Edwards said; it was night, but light shone out across the street from the saloons.)

Well, the first thing that Santa Claus said was, "Hello, Edwards!" ("Did he know you?" Mary asked, and Laura asked, "How did you know he was really Santa Claus?" Mr. Edwards said that Santa Claus knew everybody. And he had recognized Santa at once by his whiskers. Santa Claus had the longest, thickest, whitest set of whiskers west of the Mississippi.)

So Santa Claus said, "Hello, Edwards! Last time I saw you you were sleeping on a corn-shuck bed in Tennessee." And Mr. Edwards well remembered the little pair of red yarn mittens that Santa Claus had left for him that time.

Then Santa Claus said: "I understand you're living now down along the Verdigris River. Have you ever met up, down yonder, with two little girls named Mary and Laura?"

"I surely am acquainted with them," Mr. Edwards replied.

"It rests heavy on my mind," said Santa Claus. "They are both of them sweet, pretty, good little young things, and I know they are expecting me. I surely do hate to disappoint the good little girls like them. Yet with the water up the way it is, I can't ever make it across that creek. I can figure no way whatsoever to get to their cabin this year, Edwards," Santa Claus said. "Would you do me the favor to fetch their gifts this one time?"

"I'll do that, and with pleasure," Mr. Edwards told him.

Then Santa Claus and Mr. Edwards stepped across the street to the hitching posts where the pack mule was tied. ("Didn't he have his reindeer?" Laura asked. "You know he couldn't," Mary said. "There isn't any snow." "Exactly," said Mr. Edwards. Santa Claus travelled with a pack mule in the southwest.)

And Santa Claus uncinched the pack and looked through it, and he took out the presents for Mary and Laura.

"Oh, what are they?" Laura cried; but Mary asked, "Then what did he do?"

Then he shook hands with Mr. Edwards, and he swung up on his fine bay horse. Santa Claus rode well for a man of his weight and build. And he tucked his long, white whiskers under his bandanna. "So long, Edwards," he said, and he rode away on the Fort Dodge trail, leading his pack mule and whistling.

Laura and Mary were silent an instant, thinking of that.

Then Ma said, "You may look now, girls."

Something was shining bright in the top of Laura's stocking. She squealed and jumped out of bed. So did Mary, but Laura beat her to the fireplace. And the shining thing was a glittering new tin cup.

Mary had one just like it.

These new tin cups were their very own. Now they each had a cup to drink out of. Laura jumped up and down and shouted and laughed but Mary stood still and looked with shining eyes at her own tin cup.

Then they plunged their hands into the stockings again. And they pulled out two long, long sticks of candy. It was peppermint candy, striped red and white. They looked and looked at that beautiful candy, and Laura licked her stick, just one lick, just one lick. But Mary was not so greedy. She didn't even take one lick at her stick.

Those stockings weren't empty yet. Mary and Laura pulled out two small packages. They unwrapped them, and each found a little heart-shaped cake. Over their delicate brown tops was sprinkled white sugar. The sparkling grains lay like tiny drifts of snow.

The cakes were too pretty to eat. Mary and Laura just looked at them. But at last Laura turned hers over, and she nibbled a tiny nibble from underneath, where it wouldn't show. And the inside of that little cake was white!

It had been made of pure white flour, and sweetened with white sugar.

Laura and Mary never would have looked in their stockings again. The cups and the cakes and the candy were almost too much. They were too happy to speak. But Ma asked if they were sure the stockings were empty.

Then they put their arms down inside them, to make sure.

And in the toe of each stocking was a shining bright, new penny!

They had never even thought of such a thing as having a penny. Think of having a whole penny for your very own. Think of having a cup and a cake and a stick of candy and a penny.

There never had been such a Christmas.

Now of course, right away, Laura and Mary should have thanked Mr. Edwards for bringing those lovely presents all the way from Independence. But they had forgotten all about Mr. Edwards. They had even forgotten Santa Claus. In a minute they would have remem-

bered, but before they did, Ma said, gently, "Aren't you going to thank Mr. Edwards?"

"Oh, thank you, Mr. Edwards. Thank you!" they said, and they meant it with all their hearts. Pa shook Mr. Edwards' hand, too, and they shook it again. Pa and Ma and Mr. Edwards acted as if they were almost crying, Laura didn't know why. So she gazed again at her beautiful presents.

She looked up again when Ma gasped. And Mr. Edwards was taking sweet potatoes out of his pockets. He said they had helped to balance the package on his head when he swam across the creek. He thought Pa and Ma might like them with the Christmas turkey.

There were nine sweet potatoes. Mr. Edwards had brought them all the way from town, too. It was just too much. Pa said so. "It's too much, Edwards," he said. They never could thank him enough.

Mary and Laura were much too excited to eat breakfast. They drank the milk from their shining new cups, but they could not swallow the rabbit stew and the cornmeal mush.

"Don't make them, Charles," Ma said. "It will soon be dinner time."

For Christmas dinner there was the tender, juicy, roasted turkey. There were the sweet potatoes, baked in the ashes and carefully wiped so that you could eat the skins, too. There was a loaf of salt-rising bread made from the last of the white flour.

And after all that there were stewed dried blackberries and little cakes. But these little cakes were made with brown sugar and they did not have white sugar sprinkled over their tops.

Then Pa and Ma and Mr. Edwards sat by the fire and talked about Christmas times back in Tennessee and up north in the Big Woods. But Mary and Laura looked at their beautiful cakes and played with their pennies and drank water out of their new cups. And little by little they licked and sucked their sticks of candy, till each stick was sharp-pointed on one end.

That was a happy Christmas.

Day Before Christmas

By Marchette Chute

We have been helping with the cake
   And licking out the pan,
And wrapping up our packages
   As neatly as we can.
And we have hung our stockings up
   Beside the open grate,
And now there's nothing more to do
   Except
      To
         Wait!

A Piano by Christmas

By Paul Tulien

There was one thing Billy's mother had been wanting, and that was a piano. Mother liked to play, and before her marriage she had played on her sister's piano every evening.

Father wanted to buy her a piano, but Mother felt they should not spend the money. "Every month we have to make a payment on the car and a payment on the house. We have to pay the grocery bill and the milk bill and the utility bills, and occasionally a doctor bill or an insurance bill or a plumbing bill or a tax bill," Mother said. "That's enough without adding monthly payments on a piano. After we get the house paid for, we can think about it."

"We could take the money we have in the savings and loan association," Father said.

"No," Mother said. "That money is for an emergency, and the piano isn't an emergency."

Father liked to play jokes on Mother. Sometimes he would hide something he knew she would need. Then he would help her hunt for the "lost" article so that

106

A Piano by Christmas

Mother didn't suspect him, even though he had played the same trick before. When her back was turned he would put the article somewhere in plain view and call her attention to it, telling her that she must be getting blind if she couldn't see a thing right in full view.

Mother would pretend to get mad, then she and Father would laugh, and Billy would laugh too.

One day Mother received a letter from a lawyer in a distant city, informing her that an uncle whom she hardly knew had died, and that she was one of the heirs. The lawyer didn't know what Mother's share of the inheritance would be, but it might be about a thousand dollars. It might take a number of months before she would get the money, however. Time had to be given for any creditors of the estate to put in their claims.

"A thousand dollars!" Father exclaimed. "Now you can have a piano! You can get it right now. Just take out the savings and loan money, and pay it back when you get your check."

"No," Mother said. "I'll wait till I get the inheritance money." This was in the summertime, so she added, "Maybe I can get a piano by Christmas." And she did go to town the next day to pick out the piano she wanted.

One morning, another letter came from the lawyer. Mother cut open the envelope and pulled out the letter and a check.

"Is it a thousand dollars, Mom?" Billy asked eagerly.

"No, it isn't," Mother said, sounding very disappointed. "It's not half enough to buy a piano."

107

"Why isn't it more?"

Mother read the letter again. "It seems there were a lot of claims against the estate that they didn't know about before," she said. She sighed a little. "The piano will have to wait."

When Father heard about the letter and the small check he said, "Buy the piano anyway. We can make up the difference."

"No," Mother said. "I'll start a piano fund with this money, and I'll build it up with the money I earn."

"How are you going to earn money?"

"I've been thinking about that this afternoon," Mother said. "For one thing, I'll baby-sit. Perhaps I can think of other ways to make money too."

Unfortunately there seemed to be a surplus of baby sitters in the town, and the fund grew very slowly. Though Mother tried to think of other ways to earn money she could think of nothing practical then until one day in the fall, as she and Billy were carrying a pile of old magazines to the shed beside the garage, she exclaimed, "Billy, I have an idea! This shed could be useful!"

"What could we use it for?"

"A henhouse! We can ask Father to help us. I don't know anything about chickens, but he grew up on a farm. He will know!"

They told Father about the idea that evening. He said that it might work out. "Of course, a project like this won't be a gold mine," he warned. "But you should make something out of it, if you don't spend too much getting ready."

"Is there much to get ready?" Mother asked.

"You'll need some lumber for roosts and nests and a feedbox, but I can get some old crating that will do. And I'll look around for some old chicken netting to make a pen."

Within a week they had everything ready. Mother cleaned out the shed and dug the holes for posts, and in the evenings she and Father set the posts and put up the netting. Then Mother patched the holes in the netting by weaving wire back and forth. "It's like darning a sock," she said, "except that wire is stiffer and harder to handle."

As soon as the henhouse and pen were ready, Mother bought a dozen Leghorns. Father said they would be the best layers. Mother gave fresh water to the hens twice a day, and she never let the feedbox get empty. The hens rewarded her faithful care with a dozen eggs almost every day.

"Will they lay an egg a day all year round?" Mother asked.

"I'm afraid not," Father said, "but with today's better hens and better feeds they lay more than they used to. Long ago, the average hen laid fewer than a hundred eggs a year. Now a good hen should lay more than three hundred."

"Are these good hens?" Billy asked.

"I hope so," Father replied. "But sometime during this

109

fall or winter they will molt—that is, they will lose their old feathers and grow new ones. While that is going on they'll quit laying for a few weeks."

The piano fund grew faster now, especially those weeks when it wasn't necessary to buy any feed. But when a sack of mash had to be bought, there wasn't anything left to put in the fund that week. "If only hens could live on grass and bugs," Mother said wistfully.

"They could *live* on that, I suppose," Father chuckled, "though I doubt if they would lay any eggs."

Still the fund grew steadily. "I may have the piano by Christmas, after all," Mother said happily.

Then, early in November, two of the hens began to molt, and the next week several more. By mid-November Mother was only getting four or five eggs a day. "Oh dear!" she sighed. "Now when eggs are being sold for high prices I have fewer to sell."

"That's why the prices are high," Father said. "Fewer eggs are coming in. It's the old law of supply and demand."

"I'll never get the piano by Christmas now," Mother said.

"We could swing it if you'd let me help," Father said.

"No," Mother said, shaking her head. "Thank you just the same."

The next evening Mother showed Father an advertisement in the paper. "It's a medicine you mix in the feed to make hens lay," she explained. Then Father read the advertisement too. "I doubt if it would do your

110

hens any good. They're getting a balanced ration, and the only reason they aren't laying is that they're taking a rest. If their ration were lacking in certain needed minerals or vitamins, then a medicine might help."

Hiding her disappointment, Mother talked about other things. Then Father surprised her by saying, "Did you say that the medicine costs just a dollar? Perhaps it wouldn't be a bad idea to try it."

A week later Father hardly got inside the door before Mother cried, "The medicine works! I got eleven eggs today! Look!"

"Well, well! What do you know about that!" He winked at Billy and said, "Your Mother could not have been more pleased if the hens had laid diamonds."

A few evenings later Mother asked in bewilderment,

111

"Can a hen lay more than one egg in a day? Because I got eighteen eggs today!"

"When I was a boy on the farm they didn't," Father said, "but as I've said before, hens and feeds have been improved tremendously since then."

"They won't hurt themselves by laying so much, will they?" Mother asked anxiously.

Father laughed. "Don't fret about them! As soon as you get your piano they can all take a rest."

With more eggs than ever to sell at high winter prices, the piano fund now spurted upward. Mother even found more baby-sitting jobs. Women who wanted to do Christmas shopping left their children with her, and sometimes she had a half dozen boys and girls to look after.

Evenings found Mother tired but happy. "I will have the piano by Christmas for sure," she said.

On the last day of school before the Christmas vacation Billy heard piano music as he neared home! He rushed in the door, slamming it behind him. Sure enough, Mother had her piano, and she was playing it. She turned and caught Billy and hugged him. "Isn't it beautiful!" she exclaimed.

"Play some more, Mom, and I'll sing."

So Mother played "Jingle Bells" and other songs that Billy knew. And that evening, after they had eaten, Mother let the dishes go till morning. She played, and they all sang.

At last Mother asked, "What time is it?"

Father looked at his watch. "A quarter after ten."

"My goodness!" exclaimed Mother. "Billy should have been in bed long ago."

"There's one song we must sing, and then we'll all go to bed," Father said. "Play 'Silent Night'." So Mother played the old carol, and they all sang it.

The next evening Mother said, "I got only four eggs today. It's strange they should quit like that. You don't suppose the medicine has hurt them, do you?"

"It's just as I supposed all along," Father said. "They knew you wanted a piano, so they did their best to help. Now you *have* the piano, so they don't see any reason why they should keep on working so hard." Then he laughed so uproariously that Mother became very quiet.

"I smell a rat!" she said.

Billy sniffed. "I don't smell anything."

"It isn't that kind of rat, Billy. It's just an expression. It means I suspect something. I don't believe the hens laid all those eggs. Your father has been playing one of his jokes on me. Haven't you?"

And with a grin Father said, "Sure! Every day I bought some eggs, and every morning before I went to work I put them in the nests."

"Was that fair?" Mother said sternly.

"Sure it was fair," insisted Father. "I wanted to help but you wouldn't let me. All of us enjoy the piano, so there was no reason why I shouldn't help. If it hadn't been for those extra eggs, we wouldn't have had the piano by Christmas."

Then Mother gave Father a hug, and they were all happy.

A Visit From St. Nicholas

By Clement Clarke Moore

'Twas the night before Christmas, when all through the
   house
Not a creature was stirring, not even a mouse;
The stockings were hung by the chimney with care,
In hopes that *St. Nicholas* soon would be there.

The children were nestled all snug in their beds,
While visions of sugarplums danced in their heads;
And Mama in her kerchief, and I in my cap,
Had just settled our brains for a long winter's nap,

When out on the lawn there arose such a clatter,
I sprang from my bed to see what was the matter.
Away to the window I flew like a flash,
Tore open the shutters and threw up the sash.

The moon on the breast of the new-fallen snow
Gave the luster of midday to objects below;
When, what to my wondering eyes should appear,
But a miniature sleigh, and eight tiny reindeer,

With a little old driver, so lively and quick,
I knew in a moment it must be *Saint Nick*.
More rapid than eagles his coursers they came,
And he whistled and shouted, and called them by name:

"Now, *Dasher!* now, *Dancer!* now, *Prancer* and *Vixen!*
On, *Comet!* on, *Cupid!* on, *Donder* and *Blitzen!*
To the top of the porch! to the top of the wall!
Now dash away! dash away! dash away all!"

As dry leaves that before the wild hurricane fly,
When they meet with an obstacle, mount to the sky,
So up to the housetop the coursers they flew,
With the sleigh full of toys, and *St. Nicholas*, too.

116

A Visit from St. Nicholas

And then, in a twinkling, I heard on the roof,
The prancing and pawing of each little hoof.
As I drew in my head, and was turning around,
Down the chimney *St. Nicholas* came with a bound.

He was dressed all in fur, from his head to his foot,
And his clothes were all covered with ashes and soot;
A bundle of toys he had flung on his back,
And he looked like a peddler just opening his pack.

His eyes, how they twinkled! his dimples, how merry!
His cheeks were like roses, his nose like a cherry!
His droll little mouth was drawn up like a bow,
And the beard on his chin was as white as the snow;

117

The stump of a pipe he held tight in his teeth,
And the smoke, it encircled his head like a wreath;
He had a broad face and a little round belly
That shook, when he laughed, like a bowlful of jelly.

He was chubby and plump, a right jolly old elf,
And I laughed when I saw him, in spite of myself;
A wink of his eye and a twist of his head,
Soon gave me to know I had nothing to dread.

He spoke not a word, but went straight to his work,
And filled all the stockings; then turned with a jerk,
And laying his finger aside of his nose
And giving a nod, up the chimney he rose.

He sprang to his sleigh, to his team gave a whistle,
And away they all flew like the down of a thistle.
But I heard him exclaim, ere he drove out of sight,
"Happy Christmas to all, and to all a good night!"

How Santa Claus Found the Poorhouse

By Sophie Swett

Heliogabalus was shoveling snow. The snow was very deep, and the path from the front door to the road was a long one, and the shovel was almost as big as Heliogabalus.

But Gobaly—as everybody called him for short—didn't give up easily. You might have known that he wouldn't give up easily by one glance at his sturdy little figure, at his bright, wide-open eyes, his firm mouth, and his square, prominent chin; even the little, turned-up end of his nose looked resolute.

Besides, Mrs. Pynchum had told him to shovel out the path; and she had a switch behind the woodshed door, to say nothing of her slipper.

Mrs. Pynchum kept the poor farm, and Gobaly was "town's poor." The boys sometimes called him that, when he went to coast on Three-Pine Hill or to see the skating on the millpond; and sometimes, too, they made fun of his clothes. But it was only the boys who were a great deal bigger than he who dared to make fun of Gobaly,

119

and some of them even ran when he doubled up his fists. But Methuselah! I don't know what would have become of Methuselah if he had not had Gobaly to defend him. For he was a delicate little fellow; "spindlin' and good for nothin'," Mrs. Pynchum called him; and he had come to her in a basket—in other words, Methuselah was a foundling.

Mrs. Pynchum "didn't think much of children who came in a basket from nobody knew where. It didn't seem to belong to Poplarville to support him, since he didn't belong to anybody that ever lived there, and his keep and his medicine cost more than he would ever be worth to anybody."

Gobaly's mother died in the poorhouse, and left him there, a baby; she had always lived in the town, and so had his father, so of course Gobaly had a perfect right there; and old Dr. Barnacle, who was very learned, had said of him that he was an uncommonly fine baby, and had named him Heliogabalus.

Besides, he was strong and willing, and did a great deal of work. Mrs. Pynchum "could put up with Gobaly." But Methuselah, she said, was a "thorn in her side." And now, after being a trial all his life, he had a hip disease, which the doctor feared was incurable, and which made him more troublesome still!

But, after all, Mrs. Pynchum wasn't quite so bad as one would have thought from her talk. She must have had a soft spot somewhere in her heart, for she put plums in Methuselah's porridge, now that he was ill, and once she had let Gobaly leave his wood-chopping to draw him out on his sled.

I suppose there is a soft spot in everybody's heart, only sometimes it isn't very easy to find it; and Mrs. Pynchum might not have been so cross if she had led an easier life. There were a good many queer people in the poorhouse, "flighty in their heads and wearin' in their ways," she said, and sometimes they must have been trying to the patience.

Once in a great while, indeed, Mrs. Pynchum was good-natured, and then, sometimes for a whole evening, the poorhouse would seem like home. All those who lived there would then sit around the fire and roast apples; and Mrs. Pynchum would even unlock the closet under the back stairs, where there was a great bag full of nuts that Sandy Gooding and Gobaly had gathered; and Uncle Sim Perkins would tell stories.

But it happened very unfortunately that Mrs. Pynchum never had one of her good-natured days on Thanksgiving, or Christmas, or any holiday. She was sure to say on those days that she was "all tried to pieces."

And everybody was frightened and unhappy when Mrs. Pynchum was "all tried to pieces," and so that was the reason why Gobaly's heart sank as he remembered, while he was shoveling the path through the snow, that the next day was Christmas.

Some people from the village went by with a Christmas tree, which they had cut down in the woods just beyond the poorhouse; there were children in the party, and they called to Gobaly and wished him a merry Christmas, and asked him if they were going to have a Christmas tree at his house, and expressed great surprise that he wasn't going to hang up his stocking. Then one of the children suddenly exclaimed:

"Why, that's the poorhouse! It's never Christmas there!"

Poor Gobaly's heart sank still more as he caught these words, and somehow he felt very tired, and minded the cold, as he had not thought of minding it a moment before, and the snowbank looked as if he never could shovel through it. For though Gobaly was stouthearted, he didn't like to be reminded that he was "town's poor," and that Christmas was nothing to him.

Just then he caught sight of Methuselah's little pinched face pressed against the windowpane. Methuselah always had, even when he was a baby, a wan and pallid face, like a little old man, and that was why they called him Methuselah. It was cold in the front room but Methuselah had wrapped himself in a piece of an old quilt and stolen into the back room and to the window, where he could see Gobaly shoveling the snow.

Methuselah never was quite happy when Gobaly was out of his sight.

Gobaly went up to the window.

"Tomorrow's Christmas, 'Thusely!" he said.

"Is it? Do you s'pose she knows it? She'll be 'all tried to pieces,' won't she?"

("She" always meant Mrs. Pynchum in the poorhouse;
nobody there ever spoke of her in any other way.)

Gobaly was sadly afraid that she would, but he said,
cheerfully:

"Maybe she won't. Maybe she'll let me take you out
on my sled; and one Christmas there was turkey and
plum pudding."

"Must have been a good many Christmases ago; I
can't remember it!" said Methuselah. "Some folks have
'em every Christmas, Uncle Sim says, but perhaps it isn't
true. Gobaly, do you believe there really is any Santa
Claus, such as Uncle Sim tells about, or did he make it
all up? To be sure, he showed me a picture of him."

"I know there is," said Gobaly firmly, "because I've

seen presents that he brought to boys and girls in the village."

"Then why don't he ever come here and bring us some?" said Methuselah, as if a new idea had suddenly struck him. "Do you s'pose it's because we're worse than any other boys in the world? She says we are, sometimes. Or maybe he's too proud to stop at the poorhouse."

"Perhaps he can't find the way," said Gobaly. " 'Cause it's a pretty crooked road, you know. Or maybe he wouldn't think it was worth the while to come so far out of the village just for us; he wouldn't be going to Squire Thorndike's, because there aren't any children there, and there aren't any other houses on this road."

"I wish we lived where there was a truly Christmas, like places where Uncle Sim has been; don't you, Gobaly? Maybe he makes them all up, though; it seems as if they must be too good to be true."

"I shouldn't wonder if you get lots of plums in your porridge tomorrow and perhaps a piece of mince pie. And I'll ask her to let me take you up to Three-Pine Hill on the sled."

Gobaly always showed the bright side of things to Methuselah and he had become so accustomed to look-ing for a bright side that he could find one when you wouldn't have thought there was any there.

And whenever he found a very big lump in his throat he swallowed it for Methuselah's sake, and pretended that he didn't see anything in the world to cry about.

He had to go back to his shoveling then, but after he

had started he turned back to say: "When I'm a man, you shall have Christmases, 'Thusely!"

It was in that way that Gobaly often comforted Methuselah. It never seemed to occur to either of them that 'Thusely might possibly grow to be a man too.

Gobaly went to work at the snow again as if it were not a bit bigger than he was, and he soon had a rampart piled up on each side of the path so high that he thought it must look like the Chinese Wall which Uncle Sim was always telling of.

As he was digging the very last shovelful of snow out of the path, he heard the jingle of sleighbells, saw the butcher's wagon, set upon runners and drawn by a very frisky horse, going in the direction of the village. The butcher's boy and three of his comrades occupied the seat, and as many more boys were wedged in among the joints of meat and heaps of poultry in the back of the wagon. They were evidently combining pleasure with business in the liveliest manner.

Coming in the other direction, from the village, was a large Newfoundland dog with a basket in his mouth. Gobaly liked dogs, and he was sure that he was acquainted with every one in the village. As he was on intimate terms with every big one, he knew that this must be a stranger.

The butcher's boy was driving recklessly, and seemed to think it would be fun to make a sudden turn into the drifts through which the dog was bounding. The horse, taken by surprise and somewhat frightened, made a sudden plunge; and though Gobaly could not quite see how it happened, it seemed that before the dog had time to get out of the way, the sled had gone over him, and he lay helpless and howling upon the snow!

The boys either found it impossible to stop their horse, or were too frightened to investigate the extent of the mischief they had done, for they went careening on, and left the poor dog to his fate.

Gobaly was at his side in a moment, patting his shaggy black head, calling him "poor doggie" and "good doggie," and trying to discover how badly he was hurt. He came to the conclusion, after a thorough examination, that his leg was either broken or badly sprained—and Gobaly was a judge of such things. He had once doctored a rooster's lame leg, and though the rooster was never again able to mount a fence, and crowed with diminished energy, he was still able to cheer his heart by fighting the three other roosters all at once, and was likely to escape the dinner pot for a long time to come, though his gait was no longer lordly. Gobaly had also successfully treated a kitten with a sprained ankle—to say nothing of one whose tail the gobbler had nipped off. And he had seen the doctor in the village set a puppy's leg, and had carefully watched the operation.

He helped the dog along toward the house—and it was well that he was a strong and sturdy little fellow or he could not have done it—and managed at last to get the poor creature, unobserved, into the woodshed. He was very much afraid that Mrs. Pynchum, if she

should see him, would order him to leave the dog in the road, and he knew it would not do to carry him in beside the kitchen fire, as he wanted to, for Mrs. Pynchum never wanted "a dirty dog in her clean house."

Gobaly found it hard to decide whether the bone was broken or only out of place, but he made a sort of a splint, such as he had seen the doctor use upon the puppy's leg, and then wound soft cloths, wet with liniment, about it, and the dog certainly seemed relieved, and licked Gobaly's hand, and looked at him with grateful eyes.

He ventured into the house after a while, and beckoned to Methuselah to come out to the woodshed.

Methuselah was convinced that Santa Claus had sent the dog to them as a Christmas present, and his delight was unbounded.

"Of course, Santa Claus must have sent him, or why would he have come down this lonely road all by himself? And you will cure him," (Methuselah thought there was little that Gobaly couldn't do if he tried) "and perhaps she will let us keep him!"

But a sudden recollection had struck Gobaly. The dog had been carrying a basket in his mouth; there might be something in it that would tell where he came from.

Though the dog's appearance was mysterious, Gobaly was not so ready as Methuselah to accept the Santa Claus theory.

He ran out and found the basket, half buried in the snow, where it had fallen from the dog's mouth. There were several letters and papers in it addressed to "Dr. Carruthers, care of Richard Thorndike, Esq."

Dr. Carruthers was the famous New York physician who was visiting Squire Thorndike! Gobaly had heard the people in the village talking about him. The dog probably belonged to him, and had been sent to the post office for his letters.

Although he had not really believed that Santa Claus sent the dog, Gobaly did feel a pang of disappointment that they must part with him so soon. But then Mrs. Pynchum would probably not have allowed them to keep him, anyhow, and she might have had him shot because his leg was hurt. That thought consoled Gobaly, and having obtained Mrs. Pynchum's permission to carry him to his master—which was readily given, since it was the easiest way to get rid of the dog—he put a very large box, with a bed in it made of straw and soft cloth, upon his sled, and then lifted the dog gently into the box. The dog whined with pain when he was moved, but still licked Gobaly's hand, as if he understood that he was his friend and did not mean to hurt him.

Methuselah stood in the shed door, and looked after them, weeping, sadly making up his mind that Santa Claus was proud and would never come to the poorhouse.

Gobaly had never been even inside Squire Thorndike's gate before, and he went up to one of the back doors with fear and trembling; the servants at Squire Thorndike's were said to be "stuck-up," and they might not be very civil to "town's poor." But at the sight of the dog they raised a great cry, and at once ushered Gobaly into the presence of Squire Thorndike and Dr. Carruthers, that he might tell them all he knew about the accident.

Dr. Carruthers was a big, jolly-looking man, with white hair and a long white beard, just like pictures of Santa Claus. Gobaly was sure that Methuselah would think he was Santa Claus if he could see him. He evidently felt very sorry about the dog's accident, and pitied him and petted him as if he were a baby; Gobaly, who had never had so much petting in his whole life, thought the dog ought to forget all about his leg.

And then he suddenly turned to Gobaly and asked him who set the leg. Gobaly answered, modestly, that he "fixed it as well as he could because there wasn't anybody else around."

"How did you know how?" asked the doctor. And Gobaly related his experiences with the rooster and the kitten and the puppy. Dr. Carruthers looked at him steadily out of a pair of eyes that were very sharp, although very kind. Then he turned to Squire Thorndike and said "an uncommon boy." Squire Thorndike answered, and they talked together in a low tone, casting an occasional glance at Gobaly.

How Gobaly's ears did burn! He wondered what Squire Thorndike knew about him, and he thought of every prank he ever had played in his life. Gobaly was an unusually good boy, but he had played a few pranks

130

—being a boy—and he thought they were a great deal worse than they really were, because Mrs. Pynchum said so. And he imagined that Dr. Carruthers was hearing all about them, and would presently turn round and say that such a bad boy had no right to touch his dog, and that such conduct was just what he should expect of "town's poor." But instead of that, after several minutes' conversation with Squire Thorndike, he turned to Gobaly, and said:

"I want an office boy, and I think you are just the boy to suit me. How would you like to come and live with me, and perhaps, one of these days, be a doctor yourself."

Gobaly caught his breath.

To go away from Mrs. Pynchum; not to be "town's poor" any more; to learn to be a doctor! He had said once in Mrs. Pynchum's hearing that he wanted to be a doctor when he grew up, and she had said, sneeringly, that "town's poor weren't very likely to get a chance to learn to be doctors."

And now the chance had come to him! Gobaly thought it seemed too much like heaven to be anything that could happen to a mortal boy!

"Well, would you like to go?" asked the doctor again, as Gobaly could find no words to answer.

"Would I, sir? Wouldn't I!" said Gobaly, with a radiant face.

"Well, then, I will make an arrangement with the selectmen—which I have no doubt it will be easy to do—

and will take you home with me tomorrow night," said the good doctor.

But the brightness had suddenly faded from Gobaly's face. He stood with his hands thrust into his trousers pockets, gazing irresolutely at the carpet.

But it was not the carpet that Gobaly saw; it might as well have been the yellow paint of the poorhouse floors for all that he noticed of its luxurious pile and beautiful colors. It was 'Thusely's pale, pinched little face that he saw! It had risen before him even while the doctor was speaking. If he went away, who would take care of 'Thusely? And 'Thusely's heart would be broken.

"I can't go, sir; I forgot. No—no—I can't go!" said Gobaly.

Oh, what a lump there was in his throat! He had swallowed many a lump for 'Thusely's sake, but that was the very biggest one!

And then he turned and ran out of the house, without any ceremony. He knew it was rude, but that lump wouldn't stay down, and though he might be called "town's poor," he wasn't going to be called a cry-baby!

And home he ran, as fast as his legs would carry him.

That night something very unusual happened. Mrs. Pynchum went to the village to a Christmas festival. She went before dark, and the spirits of everybody in the poorhouse rose as soon as she was out of sight. Mr. Pynchum piled great logs upon the fireplace, till there was such a roaring fire as had not been there for many a long day; and he told Joe Golightly and Gobaly to go

133

down cellar and bring up as many apples as they wanted to, and he found the key of the closet where the bag of nuts was kept! And Sandy Gooding brought out some fine popcorn that he had saved up; and Joe Golightly brought out his violin, which, though some of its strings were broken and its voice was a little cracked and wheezy, could yet cheer one up wonderfully with "Bonnie Dundee" and "The Campbells Are Coming." Everybody was merry—although there was no Christmas tree, and nobody had a present except 'Thusely, who had a big red peppermint-drop that Gobaly bought him with a penny hoarded for six weeks—and it would have been a very pleasant evening if there had not been one great drawback. Mrs. Pynchum had a way of pouncing upon people when they least expected her. If a window rattled or a mouse stirred in the wall, a hush fell upon the mirth, and everybody shrank with dread. It would be so like Mrs. Pynchum to suspect that they were having a good time, and turn back to put a stop to it before she had fairly reached the festival!

Just as they had poured out a popperful of corn—popped out so big and white that it would do you good to see it—and Uncle Sim was clearing his throat to begin a story, there came a loud knock at the door. Everybody jumped. Mr. Pynchum and Sandy began to cram the apples into their pockets, and thrust the cornpopper into the closet, and Joe hid his violin under his coattails. It took them fully two minutes to remember that Mrs. Pynchum never knocked.

Mr. Pynchum sat down again, and said, in a tone of surprise, as if he had not been in the least agitated: "What is the matter with you all? Gobaly, open the door."

Gobaly opened the door, and who should be there but Squire Thorndike and the city doctor!

The moment 'Thusely saw Dr. Carruthers he called out "Santa Claus!" And the big doctor laughed, and took a great package of candy out of his pocket and gave it to 'Thusely.

After that it was of no use for Gobaly to whisper, "The dog gentleman!" in 'Thusely's ear; he couldn't think it was anybody but Santa Claus.

"I'm so glad you've come!" he said, confidentially. "And you look just like your picture. And I don't see why you never came before, for you don't seem proud. And we aren't such very bad boys; anyway, Gobaly isn't. Don't you believe what Mrs. Pynchum tells you! Will you?"

The doctor laughed, and said he was getting to be an old fellow, and the snow was deep, and it was hard for him to get about; but he was sorry he hadn't come before, for he thought they did look like good boys. Then he asked Methuselah about his lameness and the pain in his side, and said he ought to be sent to a certain hospital in New York, where he might be cured. And then he asked if he had no relatives or friends.

"I've got Gobaly," said 'Thusely.

The doctor turned and looked sharply at Gobaly.

"Is he the reason why you wouldn't go with me?" he asked.

"He's such a little chap, and I'm all he's got," said Gobaly.

The doctor took out his handkerchief and said it was bad weather for colds.

"Suppose I take him, too?" said he.

This time the lump in his throat fairly got the better of Gobaly!

But 'Thusely clapped his hands for joy. He didn't understand what was to happen, only that Santa Claus was to take him somewhere with Gobaly; and one thing that 'Thusely was sure of was that he wanted to go wherever Gobaly went. And he kept saying:

"I told you that Santa Claus sent the dog—now, didn't I, Gobaly?"

Methuselah went to the hospital and was cured, and Gobaly—well, if I should tell you his name, you might say that you had heard of him as a famous surgeon-doctor. I think it is probable that he could now make a lame rooster or a kitten with a sprained ankle just as good as new, and I am sure he wouldn't be above trying; for he has a heart big enough to sympathize with any creature that suffers.

There is at least one person in the world who will agree with me, and that is a gentleman who was once a miserable little cripple in a poorhouse, and was called Methuselah.

Golden Cobwebs

(An Old Tale Retold in Verse)

By Rowena Bennett

The Christmas tree stood by the parlor door,
  But the parlor door was locked
And the children could not get inside
  Even though they knocked.
For a Christmas tree must wait, folks say,
And not be seen till Christmas Day.
But the cat had seen the Christmas tree
  As she prowled the house by night,
And the dog had seen the Christmas tree
  By the moon's enchanting light;
And a little mouse beside her hole
Had looked at it with eyes of coal.
Even the spiders hoped to see
The secret, silent Christmas tree.

They planned, one day, to creep and crawl
Out of their cracks and up the wall
To get the highest view of all.
But just that day with mop and broom
The housemaid swept them from the room
And so the spiders could not see
The secret, silent Christmas tree.

The fairies heard the spiders weep,
    All on a winter's night,
Although their cries made softer sounds
    Than moth wings make in flight.
The fairies said: "Each living thing
That creeps, or crawls, or flaps a wing
Shall share the birthday of the King."

They took the spiders to the tree
    And, since they were too small
To see as far as cat or mouse,
    The fairies let them crawl
Along each twig and bending branch
    To look at every ball
And silver star and popcorn string;
And when they had seen everything
They thanked the fairies and went back
Each one to sleep inside his crack.

But, oh, the tree when they were gone
Was very sad to look upon!

Golden Cobwebs

Its branches were more gray than green
And little webs hung in between
That dulled the lights and all the sheen.

The fairies shook their heads and sighed,
For in their wisdom, ever wide,
They knew no housewife cared to see
Dull cobwebs on a Christmas tree.
They knew the children, too, would weep
To waken from their yuletide sleep
And glimpse a tree all bearded gray
That would not shine on Christmas Day....

And so they turned the webs to gold
By waving fairy wands, I'm told;
And that is why there'll always be
Bright cobwebs on a Christmas tree.

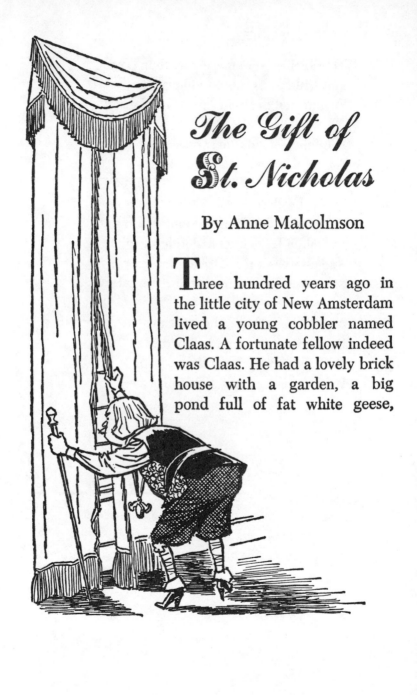

The Gift of St. Nicholas

By Anne Malcolmson

Three hundred years ago in the little city of New Amsterdam lived a young cobbler named Claas. A fortunate fellow indeed was Claas. He had a lovely brick house with a garden, a big pond full of fat white geese, a thriving trade, and a pretty wife whose name was Anitje. He had worked hard for these blessings from the first bleak day when he landed on the shores of the New World, an orphan boy from Holland. He was now a rich man, rich enough to wear eight pairs of breeches at once.

The only dark cloud in his sky was Roeloffsen, the burgomaster, an old miser who had long been in love with Anitje. As the richest old bachelor in the town, he had expected her to marry him without question. When she married the poor cobbler boy, the burgomaster's pride was hurt. He swore that he should have his revenge. Whenever Claas and Anitje walked out in their Sunday clothes, their family of fat Dutch children toddling behind them, he hid behind the heavy curtains of his house and said terrible things.

At last his ugly thoughts were put into deeds. He taught the village blacksmith to make hobnails for the townspeople's boots. These nails made a dreadful racket as they clattered over the brick streets. But they kept the boots from wearing out. The boots wore so long that poor Claas had very little business as a cobbler. He had a very hard time to make ends meet.

This was not enough for the black-hearted burgomaster, however. Claas and his Anitje still lived in their fine brick house and walked out Sundays in their handsome clothes. Roeloffsen had to think of something else.

Soon he knew what to do. As an officer of the city, he ordered a new street to be built. This street ran right

141

through the middle of Claas's pond. The city builders came and drained the pond. Poor Claas had to sell his beloved geese. This was a great blow to him, because the eggs he sold at the market place helped make up for the boots he was unable to sell.

But this was not the worst of it. As Claas sat by his fire sorrowing for the loss of his geese, he had visitors. These were men from the city council. Since the road ran through his land, they said, he should pay for its building. They demanded fifty pieces of gold for this purpose. Fifty pieces of gold! That was all Claas had tucked away in his teapot.

Claas and Anitje had to work harder than ever to keep their family fed and clothed. They sold vegetables from their garden and managed to make themselves a fair living. Then came the jealous burgomaster. He built another road, through the middle of Claas's garden patch this time. Once again the poor cobbler had to rob his teapot in order to pay for this road.

And so it went. Every time Claas made a little money, the burgomaster built a new road and made him pay for it. Before long he had to sell his fine house. No longer could he afford to wear eight pairs of breeches, nor Anitje her twelve petticoats. The little family was poor. They had sold all their belongings except a bare few. They lived in a miserable little cottage with only a dirt floor.

The wicked old burgomaster at last was satisfied. He danced with joy when he saw how low the cobbler had fallen. This would show the people of New Amsterdam that no orphan boy could outdo the wealthy Heer Roeloffsen!

On Christmas Eve, as the burgomaster was enjoying his fine dinner, Claas and Anitje and their children sat huddled before the fireplace in their little cottage. The very last log burned on the hearth and gave out little heat at best. Their cupboard, like old Mother Hubbard's, was bare. After their supper of bread and cheese, not a crumb remained. A poor Christmas this would be. No presents, no blazing fire, not even a dinner.

Of all their possessions, only two treasures remained. One was the Bible which Claas's mother had given him long ago. It was bound in a beautiful leather and held shut with silver clasps. Claas was tempted to take off these clasps and sell them. They might bring him enough money to provide a Christmas for his children.

"No!" said Anitje. To sell the clasps from a Bible would be wicked. He should never think of doing such a thing. Better it would be to starve than to feast on the sale of holy things.

The other treasure which remained was a pipe. This was a special, lovely pure meerschaum pipe which to Claas had a magic meaning. As a little boy, leaving his home for the New World, he had found the pipe in his stocking. Where it had come from he could not tell. He was sure it was a present from the good Saint Nicholas himself.

As he rubbed it the cottage door swung open and a

blast of cold air filled the room. There before the fire stood a fat little stranger, about three feet tall. He was dripping with snow, and icicles hung from his shaggy eyebrows and long white beard.

"Br-r-r!" muttered the stranger crossly. "It's a wonder you wouldn't answer the door when a traveler knocks. Fine manners, I must say, on a night like this!"

All thoughts of the pipe were forgotten as Claas and Anitje stared at their visitor. The children scrambled to hide under the bed. Only their blue eyes shone out from behind the curtains.

"Well, come along! Come along!" went on the visitor, growing more angry every minute. "Don't stand there! The least you can do is to put another log on the fire so that I can warm myself. Can't you see I'm half frozen?"

"I-I-I-I'm very sorry, sir," admitted Claas, finding his tongue at last, "but there is not another log to put on the fire. You're very welcome to warm yourself at our poor hearth."

"Well, then," snapped the stranger, "send one of those ragamuffins out to the woodshed. I'm freezing, I tell you!" He glared at the children, who pushed themselves farther back under the bed hangings.

"Oh sir!" cried Anitje, "if only we had more wood in the shed we would gladly fetch it for you. But alas, this is our last stick. We have no more to keep ourselves warm."

"Humph!" snorted the little fellow. "That's very careless of you. But what must be, must be!" With that he cracked the fine cane he carried over his knee. It broke into several pieces. These he tossed onto the coals. As they struck the fire, something wonderful happened. Each of the pieces of cane changed into a big birch log. The dark coals blazed up and soon the room was dancing with the light of a huge fire.

"That's better," muttered the stranger. "Upon my life, I thought I should turn into an icicle for all you cared."

The children crept out of their hiding place to gape at the magic blaze. Claas and Anitje rubbed their eyes.

"And now, I suppose, you're going to let me starve to death, too!" sneered the visitor, looking in the direction of the cupboard. "It's a wonder you wouldn't invite me to have some supper. I haven't eaten since this morning."

Tears came to Anitje's eyes. "Oh sir, whoever you may be, we would indeed be happy to give you our last crumb. But," she sobbed, "we have nothing to eat in the house. We ate our last scrap of cheese for our evening meal."

"That was certainly rude of you," barked the funny little man. "Here I come, after a hard day's tramp over the mountains, through wind and rain and snow! You say you have no bread to feed me! My dear lady, I know better. Your shelves are heaped with cakes and apples. And if that's not roast goose I smell cooking, I'll eat my beard!"

Without thinking, the whole family stopped to sniff. Why, they did smell roast goose! And cabbage and onion and mince pie and pumpkin! These delicious smells were fairly bursting from the oven door. They looked quickly at the cupboard. Its shelves were groaning under bowls of apples and pears and platters of cakes and cookies. The water jug was filled to the brim with sweet cider.

"Don't stand there, don't stand there like a forest of trees!" shouted the stranger. "Can't you see I'm dying of hunger? Get me something to eat and be quick about it. No food indeed! Why, there's a whole feast in that oven. Put it on the table."

Not knowing whether to be overjoyed or frightened, Claas and Anitje set the table and drew it before the fire. They opened the wide door of the oven. There indeed were the goose and the vegetables and the pies they smelled.

At the sight of the richly-spread table, the children forgot their shyness. Hungrily they feasted. But none of them ate so much as did their visitor. Time and again he passed back his plate for another drumstick. An ordinary goose has only two legs, but this one sprouted a new one whenever the little man passed his plate.

When at last the fat little stranger had had enough and the buttons began to burst from Claas's coat, the table was cleared away. No longer did the visitor snap angrily at his hosts. He leaned back in his chair and lit his pipe. A twinkle appeared in his eye and he patted the children's blond heads. For an hour he sat talking pleasantly with the happy family, telling them strange and marvelous tales of distant lands. But not once did he tell them who he was.

At the stroke of midnight he got up from his chair. "I must be off!" he exclaimed. "Thank you indeed for a

pleasant evening and a delicious dinner." He turned to Claas. "Don't ever sell that pipe," he shouted.

In the morning Claas was awakened by a great hammering at his door. There was Burgomaster Roeloffsen and a party of soldiers. "We have come to arrest you!" they screamed. "You are a wizard, a witch, a magician. You are a disgrace to the city of New Amsterdam."

Poor Claas didn't know what to make of it. Why

should anyone call him a wizard. He was nothing but a poor cobbler who had had a lovely dream.

"Come!" roared the burgomaster. "Open the door and let us in. We shall have no wizards in our city!"

As he slowly wakened, Claas looked about him. The wretched little cottage had disappeared. He was standing in the door of a great house. The walls were hung with silk, and from the cupboards shone silver platters and copper bowls. He looked timidly out of the window. Around him spread wide lawns and gardens and in the distance glimmered the ice of a huge pond.

"Open up, I say," bellowed the burgomaster. "Open up in the name of the law. We have come to take you to jail as you deserve." Claas opened the door. In poured the soldiers.

"Aha!" screamed Heer Roeloffsen, his face red with anger. "Seize him! Seize the witch! He has not only changed his cottage to a fine estate. He has filled his chests with gold."

Before the astonished Claas the burgomaster lifted the lid of a chest. The great box was full to the top with pieces of money.

"You thief! You robber! I'll..." But before he could finish his sentence, a pair of invisible hands clapped themselves over his mouth. More hands which could not be seen grabbed the soldiers. Then came an awful whacking and thrashing as the unseen arms paddled the burgomaster and his party with unseen switches.

"Ouch! Help! Stop it!" yelled Roeloffsen. But the

paddling went on. The soldiers ran down the path to the main road and headed away from town, crying and yelling and trying to defend themselves from the blows of the unseen paddlers.

That was the last ever seen of the jealous burgomaster. Claas and his family lived on in their fine new home, never wanting for food or warmth. How their good fortune had come they did not know. The only clue they had was a piece of paper slipped under the door. It said simply, "Don't ever sell that pipe."

A NEW SONG

By Ernest Rhys

We will sing a new song
That sounds like the old:
      Noel.

We will tell an old tale
That has often been told:
      Noel.

We will build a tall town;
We will watch for the Star:
      Noel.

We will build a new world,
  Without War.